Dirty Bertie

SLURPS and BURPS

DAVID ROBERTS WRITTEN BY ALAN MACDONALD

Collect all the Dirty Bertie books!

Worms!
Fleas!
Pants!
Burp!
Yuck!
Crackers!
Bogeys!
Mud!
Germs!
Loo!
Fetch!
Fangs!
Kiss!
Ouch!
Pong!
Pirate!
Scream!
Zombie!

Smash!
Rats!
Horror!
Jackpot!
Aliens!
Fame!
My Joke Book
My Book of Stuff

A Trio of Trouble
Mayhem and Mischief
Stinky Stories
A Dollop of Disaster

Dirty Bertie
Sticker and Activity Book
Pant-tastic
Sticker and Activity Book

Contents

STRIPES PUBLISHING
An imprint of Little Tiger Press
1 The Coda Centre, 189 Munster Road,
London SW6 6AW

A paperback original
First published in Great Britain in 2016

ISBN: 978-1-84715-712-6

A CIP catalogue record for this book is available from the British Library.

Printed and bound in the UK.

10 9 8 7 6 5 4 3 2 1

Dirty Bertie
SNOW!

For Jane – without whom there wouldn't be a series ~ A M and D R

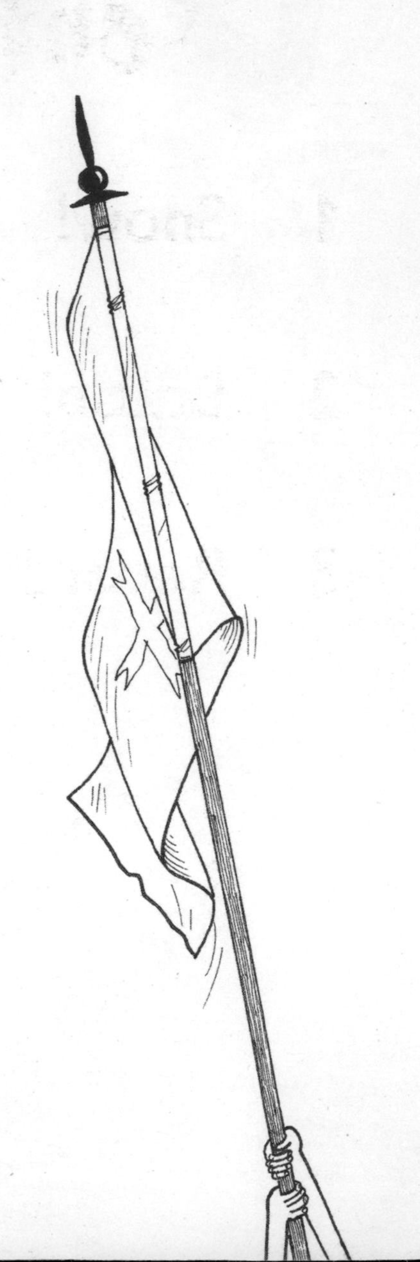

Contents

SNOW!

CHAPTER 1

Bertie woke up. He pulled back the curtains and gasped. SNOW! For weeks he'd been praying for snow and now it had finally come. Whoopee! Snowmen! Snowball fights! And even better, sledging on Pudsley Hill!

He burst into his parents' bedroom. "IT'S SNOWING!" he yelled.

"Uhh ... what?" mumbled Mum.

"It's snowing! Look outside!" shouted Bertie, pulling back the curtains.

Dad squinted at the alarm clock and groaned. "Bertie, it's not even six o'clock!"

"But it's snowing!" said Bertie.

"I don't care – go back to bed!"

Bertie went. A moment later his head poked round the door. "Do you think school will be closed?" he asked.

"BACK TO BED!" bellowed Dad.

But Bertie was too excited – how could anyone sleep when it was snowing outside? He hurried downstairs.

"Hey, Whiffer! Look, it's snowing!"

They stood at the window watching the snow coming down. There was snow on the rooftops and snow carpeting the lawn. Bertie looked at Whiffer...

Five minutes later they were in the garden. Bertie bounded around, chased excitedly by Whiffer. Snowflakes fell on his face and melted on his tongue. He scooped up a big ball of snow. *If only Darren and Eugene were here,* he thought, *we could have a snowball fight.*

CRUMP! His snowball thudded against the side of the shed.

"BERTIE!"

Uh oh. Mum stuck her head out of the back door.

"What on earth are you doing?" she cried.

"Playing," replied Bertie.

"You're still in your pyjamas! They'll get soaked!"

Bertie looked down. It was true, his pyjamas had got a little bit soggy.

"I'm wearing boots," he said.

"For heaven's sake, come in before you catch your death!"

Bertie drooped inside, trailing wet footprints through the kitchen. Whiffer shook himself, showering snow everywhere.

"Ugh!" said Mum. "Look at you, Bertie, you're wet through!"

"It's only snow," said Bertie.

"Go and get some clothes on."

In his bedroom Bertie quickly pulled on his jeans and thumped downstairs.

The phone was ringing in the hall.

"Yes?" he said, snatching up the receiver.

"Hey, Bertie!" It was Darren. "Have you heard? School's closed!"

Bertie did a wild dance of joy. "We can have snowball fights!" he whooped.

"And go sledging!" cried Darren.

"I'll meet you at Pudsley Hill," said Bertie. "Tell Eugene."

"Okay. Bring your sledge!" said Darren.

Bertie slammed down the phone. This was going to be the greatest day ever. No school, no mean old Miss Boot – he could spend the whole day playing in the snow.

Wait a moment, though. Bertie gulped. Didn't his sledge accidentally get broken last year when they tried it with four people? Argh! Disaster! He had to find a sledge and fast.

"Guess what? School's closed!" cried Bertie, scooting into the kitchen.

Dad groaned. Suzy cheered.

"Can I go sledging with my friends?" asked Bertie.

Mum sighed. "After breakfast."

"And can we get a new sledge?"

"Certainly not," said Dad.

"But ours is broken!" moaned Bertie.

"And whose fault is that?" said Mum.

"It wasn't mine. I *told* Darren he was too heavy."

"Well, we're not wasting money on sledges so you can break them," said Mum. "If you're that desperate, go and ask your gran."

"Why, is she going sledging?"

"I mean, ask if she's got a sledge. I'm sure she used to have one."

CHAPTER 2

Gran was still in her dressing gown when Bertie knocked on her door.

"Bertie!" she said. "Shouldn't you be at school?"

"SCHOOL'S CLOSED!" whooped Bertie. "IT'S SNOWING!"

"So I see," said Gran. "You'd better come in."

Bertie stamped his boots on the mat. "I've got the whole day off," he panted. "And me and my friends are going sledging, only there's one problem – we don't have a sledge."

"Oh dear," said Gran. "So what are you going to do?"

"I was hoping you'd got one," said Bertie.

"A sledge?" Gran frowned. "I think I did have one somewhere. It belonged to your dad."

"But you kept it?" asked Bertie hopefully.

"Well, I don't remember throwing it out."

"Great! Then can I borrow it – I mean, if you're not using it?"

Gran smiled. "I'm not right now,"

she said. "Wait while I get dressed and we'll have a look in the shed."

Gran's shed was so full of junk it was difficult to get in the door. Bertie stared at the jumble of deckchairs, boxes and rusty lawnmowers. Gran waded in and began to hunt through the piles of stuff. Finally she found what she was looking for.

"There! I knew it was here somewhere," she said.

Bertie stared, boggle-eyed. The sledge looked like something out of the Stone Age! It was made of heavy planks of wood nailed together. At the front was a bit of knotted old rope for steering. It smelled of mould.

"Your dad used to love this sledge!" said Gran, brushing off a cobweb.

"Really?" said Bertie. In the old days sledges must have been rubbish. Today they were light and fast, and you didn't need a team of huskies to pull them.

"What do you think?" said Gran.

"Oh, um ... yeah. Thanks, Gran!" said Bertie, trying to sound enthusiastic.

At least it was a sledge, and right now it was better than nothing.

Bertie dragged the sledge down the street. By now all his friends would be up at Pudsley Hill. As he turned the corner a boy came out of a shop with his mum, pulling a sledge behind him. Bertie's heart sank. It was Know-All Nick – the last person on earth he wanted to see.

"Oh, hello, Bertie!" he sneered.

"Hello," said Bertie coldly.

Bertie had never met Nick's mum before. She looked exactly like him, pale and neat with a long, snooty nose. She stared at Bertie as if he had fleas.

"And who is this, Nicholas?" she said. "One of your school-friends?"

"No, this is Bertie," said Nick with a sickly grin. "Going to Pudsley Hill?"

"I might be," said Bertie.

"I've got a new sledge," boasted Nick. "It's a Speedster 2000. Isn't it a beauty?"

Bertie stared. It was the sledge of his dreams – curved and sleek, with steel runners and go-faster stripes down the side. Trust Nick to have the best sledge you could buy.

"Mummy said I could have any one I liked, didn't you, Mummy?" he simpered.

"Of course I did, bunnikins."

Nick flushed pink.

"Anyway, I better be going," said Bertie. "My friends will be waiting for me."

"Yes, come along, Nicholas," said Nick's mum. But Nick had other ideas.

"HA HA!" he hooted. "IS THAT YOUR SLEDGE?"

Bertie scowled. "It's my gran's. And it's faster than it looks."

"Yeah?" said Nick. "Where did you get it from – a joke shop?"

"Don't be rude, Nicholas," tutted Nick's mum. "Come along."

"Bye, Bertie!" grinned Know-All Nick. "See you on the hill – if your sledge makes it that far!"

CHAPTER 3

By the time Bertie arrived, the hill was packed with children. Screams of laughter rang out. Sledges whizzed down the steep slope.

Eugene and Darren were waiting for him, idly throwing snowballs.

"What kept you so long?" asked Eugene.

"And what do you call THAT?" asked Darren.

"A sledge," said Bertie. "I borrowed it from my gran."

"But where's your old one?"

"If you remember, you helped break it," said Bertie. "This is the best I could do."

Darren shook his head. "That's going to be rubbish," he said.

"It smells," said Eugene, holding his nose.

Bertie rolled his eyes. "Well, get your own sledge if you're so fussy!" he said. "Anyway, it's better than it looks."

They tried a practice run. It took both Darren and Eugene to launch the sledge with Bertie on board. It trundled gently at first then gained a little speed, bumping and bouncing down the hill like an old pram. Bertie clambered off and rubbed his bottom. It was even worse than he'd thought.

"OH, BERTIE! BERTIE!"

Bertie turned round and groaned. That was all he needed – Angela Nicely. Angela lived next door to Bertie and was always telling everyone that he was her boyfriend. She had her friends Laura and Maisie with her.

"Look, Bertie! We're making a snowman!" she sang excitedly.

The snowman had a fat, lumpy body and was already taller than Angela. It stood at the foot of the slope, looking up the hill with its two coal eyes. Sledges whizzed past on either side.

"You can't build it there!" said Bertie.

"Why not?" said Angela.

"It's in the way!"

"No it's not!"

"Yes it is. We're sledging here," said Bertie. "You'll have to move it!"

"*You* move," said Angela, sticking out her tongue. "It's our snowman and we were here first."

Bertie shrugged. "Okay, but don't say I didn't warn you."

ZOOOOOM!

Something streaked past them in a blur of speed.

Know-All Nick skidded to a halt on his Speedster 2000 and got off.

"Whoo-hoo! See that?" he whooped. "That was lightning!"

"We're making a snowman!" cried Angela.

Nick ignored her. "Oh, look, it's Bertie with his grandma's sledge," he jeered.

"Ha ha," said Bertie. "Actually, it's a lot faster than it looks."

Nick smirked. "That old crate?"

"It's better than yours."

"Oh yeah?" Nick folded his arms. "Well, if you're so sure, let's have a race. First one to the bottom of the hill."

"You're on," said Bertie.

Angela clapped her hands. "Goodie! A race! I'll be the judge."

Bertie trudged up the hill, dragging the sledge behind him. He was already wishing he'd kept his big mouth shut. He flopped down on the snow beside Darren and Eugene and told them the bad news.

"A race?" said Eugene. "Are you mad?"

"He was showing off," said Bertie. "What else could I have done?"

"But a race…? Have you *seen* his sledge?"

"Tell him you changed your mind," said Darren.

"I can't, not now," said Bertie. "I'll look stupid."

"You'll look even more stupid when you lose," said Darren.

"You never know," said Bertie. "I *might* win."

"On that old heap?" said Darren. "You'd be faster in a wheelbarrow."

CHAPTER 4

The two sledges lined up at the top of the hill. Word had got round about the Great Sledge Race and a crowd from school gathered to watch. Eugene was in charge of starting the race. At the bottom of the hill, Angela Nicely waited to wave her hanky when the winner crossed the finish.

"Want me to give you a head start, Bertie?" smirked Know-All Nick.

"No thanks," said Bertie.

The two rivals got ready. Bertie lay on his front, to give his sledge extra speed.

Nick sat back on the Speedster 2000, looking smugly confident. This was going to be so easy, he wouldn't even need to cheat. He couldn't wait to see Bertie's face when he beat him by miles.

Bertie gripped the rope tight between his hands. "Ready?" he asked.

"Any time you like, slowcoach," drawled Nick.

Darren crouched down, ready to push Bertie off. Trevor did the same for Nick.

Eugene raised his arm.

"After three," he said. "Three … two … one … GO!"

Darren launched the heavy wooden sledge with all his might. It lurched forward and caught the slope, starting to bump down the hill. Bertie hung on tight. Snow kicked in his face, almost blinding him. But he was in the lead – there was no sign of that show-off Nick. He must have got a slow start.

I can win this, thought Bertie. *Just keep going and…*

WHOOOOOOOOOOSH!

Something zoomed past, showering him with snow. Bertie gaped. The Speedster 2000 whizzed down the hill like a rocket-powered missile. Bertie tried to urge Gran's old sledge to go faster, but he might as well have got off and walked.

Nick grinned. The race was in the bag. He was way out in front. He turned round to see how far behind Bertie was.

"What's the matter, loser?" he yelled. "Can't you go—"

WHUMPF!

Nick never saw the giant snowman.One minute he was racing down the hill, and the next he was flying through the air like a human cannonball.

KADOOF! He landed head first in a big pile of snow.

ZOOOOOOM!

Bertie's wooden sledge flew by, passing Angela Nicely and crossing the finish before spinning to a stop. Bertie jumped off and leaped in the air.

"YES! I WON! I WON!" he yelled.

At the top of the hill Darren, Eugene and the rest of the crowd were cheering.

Bertie hurried over to where Nick was struggling in the snow like a beetle on its back. He pulled him out.

"ARGHH! BLECH!" spluttered Nick, wiping his eyes.

"Oh dear, Nick, you're a bit wet!" Bertie grinned.

"YOU CHEATED!" gasped Nick.

Bertie shook his head. "You said first to the bottom of the hill. I was first."

"But … but… IT'S NOT FAIR!" wailed Nick, stamping his foot with rage. "You just wait, I'm going to—"

SPLAT! A big snowball hit Nick right on the ear.

"THAT'S HIM! HE WRECKED OUR SNOWMAN!" yelled Angela Nicely.

"GET HIM!"

SPLAT! SPLAT!

Snowballs pelted Nick from all sides, as Laura and Maisie joined in the attack.

Bertie grinned. There was nothing better than a snowball fight – especially when the target was snooty-nosed Nick.

He stooped down to grab a fistful of snow. It was turning into the perfect day.

BATTLE!

CHAPTER 1

Bertie watched his dad through the window. He was marching up and down the garden with a rake over his shoulder.

"What's he doing?" he asked.

Mum rolled her eyes. "Your father's joined the Black-Axe Battle Society. Grown men playing at soldiers. Can you imagine it?"

Bertie could. It sounded brilliant.

"You mean they fight REAL battles?" he said excitedly.

"No!" snorted Mum. "It's all pretend. Running round in silly hats, waving swords."

Bertie watched his dad take aim at a flowerpot. A battle club? Why hadn't anyone told him before? He was brilliant at fighting, and what's more he already had his own pirate costume.

Over supper he tried to find out more about it.

"Dad, you know this battle club you're in?" he said.

"It's not a battle club," said Dad. "It's a historical society."

Mum pulled a face at Suzy.

"But you fight battles?" said Bertie.

"We *stage* battles," corrected Dad. "It's history, Bertie. We bring history to life."

Bertie sucked up a loop of spaghetti. "And you dress up?" he said.

"We wear costumes, yes."

"And fight with swords?"

"Not just swords – we have all kinds of weapons," said Dad.

Bertie thought for a moment. "So if I came, could I be a pirate?"

Dad gave a heavy sigh. "It's nothing to do with pirates, Bertie. It's the English Civil War – the Royalists against the Roundheads."

"Why are they round heads?"

"It's just a nickname. The Royalists were on the King's side, the Roundheads fought against them."

"I'd be on the King's side," decided Bertie. "Actually, I wouldn't mind being King myself."

"You won't be anything because you're not coming," said Dad.

Bertie gaped. "Why not?"

"Yes, why not?" said Mum. "If you can play at soldiers, why can't Bertie?"

"Because it's not a game!" cried Dad crossly. "We train every week like a real army. We have to obey orders."

"We do that at school," said Bertie.

"Anyway, I'm not letting you near a battlefield," said Dad. "There'll be guns and cannons – all kinds of dangerous things."

"Cannons?" gasped Bertie. "Brilliant! *Please* can I come?"

"No," said Dad firmly. "And don't go on because I won't change my mind."

Mum cleared away the plates. "Well, I think you're being very mean," she sniffed. "Bertie would make a very good pirate."

Dad put his head in his hands. "IT'S NOTHING TO DO WITH PIRATES!"

CHAPTER 2

On Wednesday night Dad went to battle practice. When he returned, Bertie was in the lounge watching TV with Mum and Suzy. Whiffer was sprawled out on the floor.

There was a clanking in the hall and Dad appeared in the doorway.

"Well, what do you think?" he said.

"Good grief!" said Mum. "Did you walk home like that?"

Bertie stared. His dad was wearing a tin helmet that looked like a pudding bowl. Long boots flapped around his knees and he seemed to have lost the bottom half of his trousers. In his hand was an enormous pole tipped with a sharp blade.

"Wow! Is that your axe?" said Bertie impressed.

"It's called a pike," said Dad. "I'm a pikeman in the royal army."

"You look like you're in the circus," said Mum. "Be careful with that thing."

"Can I have a go?" begged Bertie.

Dad shook his head. "No, it's not for children."

"Please," said Bertie. "I just want to see what it's like."

"Oh, let him have a go," sighed Mum.

"Well, all right," said Dad, "but just for a moment, and don't go poking anyone in the eye."

Bertie jumped up eagerly. He'd never held a pike before.

It would be brilliant for poking people in the bottom. Know-All Nick for instance.

"Not like that," said Dad. "You need both hands. One up here to steady it. Got it?"

"Yes," said Bertie.

"You're sure?"

"I'm fine!" said Bertie. "Let go!"

Dad let go. The pike was a lot heavier than Bertie had expected. It started to fall.

"LOOK OUT!" cried Mum, ducking out of the way. Bertie heaved and managed to jerk the pole back upright.

CLANG! SMASH! TINKLE!

There was the sound of breaking glass and the light went out. Bertie stumbled over something in the dark, lost his grip on the pike and dropped it with a thump.

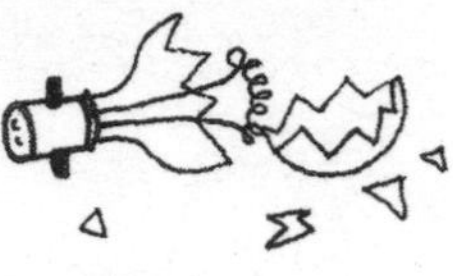

WOOF! WOOF!

"BERTIE!" yelled Mum.

"It's all right," cried Bertie. "It's only Whiffer. I trod on his tail."

Once they'd cleared up the bits of glass, Dad replaced the broken light.

"It wasn't my fault!" repeated Bertie for the tenth time.

Mum glared at Dad. "It's you I blame," she said.

"ME?" said Dad.

"It's your stupid spear!"

"It's not a spear," said Dad. "It's a pike."

"I don't care what it is, don't bring it in the house!"

"I've got to practise for Saturday," argued Dad.

"And that's another thing," said Mum. "I'm taking Suzy shopping on Saturday."

Dad's mouth fell open. "But that's the day of my first battle. What about Bertie?"

"I'm not dragging him round the shops with us," said Mum. "Last time I took him to Dibble's, he jumped in a lift and ended up on the fifth floor!"

"Who's going to look after him, then?" asked Dad.

"You are!"

"I can't! I'll be fighting the battle."

"Well, surely Bertie can go and watch?" said Mum.

"Yes! Can I, Dad?" begged Bertie.

Dad looked at him wearily. "If you must," he sighed.

Bertie whooped.

"But you're only coming to watch," warned Dad. "You are NOT taking part."

CHAPTER 3

Saturday morning dawned. Bertie chattered excitedly to Dad all the way to the battlefield. When they arrived, he stared … where was the battle? He had expected two great armies with banners and knights in armour. Instead there was a scattering of tents at the foot of a hill. People were strolling around dressed in long boots and floppy hats.

"Right," said Dad, locking the car and heading for a white tent. "You wait outside while I go and sign in. And don't wander off or touch anything."

"I won't," promised Bertie. He stood outside the tent watching some soldiers who were smoking pipes round a fire.

After ten minutes he noticed a queue had formed behind him.

"Right, who's next?" asked a big, bearded man, appearing from the tent.

"What's your name, lad?"

"Who me?" said Bertie.

"Well you're in the queue. What's your name?"

"Bertie. Bertie Burns."

The man checked his list. "You're not down here," he said. "Never mind, who are you with?"

"My dad," said Bertie.

"No, I mean whose side are you on? Parliament or the King?"

"Oh, I'm for the King," said Bertie.

"Good lad," said the man. "Well, as it happens, the King's army is short of a drummer boy – how does that sound?"

Bertie's face lit up. "Brilliant. Oh, but I haven't got a drum."

"Don't worry about that," said the man. "Pop into the tent and see Sarah, she'll kit you out with a uniform."

Bertie hurried inside. He couldn't believe his luck. He was actually going to take part in the battle. Wait till his dad heard about this!

A short time later he emerged from the tent wearing a black jacket, a flat hat and baggy velvet bloomers. A large blue drum hung at his side. Bertie banged it a few times to see what kind of noise it made. The soldiers round the fire looked up and glared.

Just then Dad appeared. "Bertie! Where have you been?" he cried. He stared. "What's that?"

"It's a drum," said Bertie.

"Yes, but what are you doing with it?"

"I'm a drummer boy in the army. Listen to this," said Bertie.

He played a deafening drum roll. BRRRRRRRRRR…

"STOP!" yelled Dad. "I thought I made it clear you *weren't* in the battle?"

"It wasn't my fault! They needed a drummer!" said Bertie.

They were interrupted by a red-faced man trotting over on an enormous horse. He seemed to be having trouble controlling it.

"Ah, Burns!" he boomed. "All set? Looking forward to the battle, eh?"

"I was," sighed Dad. "When do we start?"

"Not long," said the man. "We'll be on the right flank, defending the hill with Prince Percy. Pikemen at the front, of course."

Bertie raised his hand. "Where do I go?" he asked.

"Oh, this is my son, Bertie," explained Dad. "This is Sir Harry Crackpot, General of the King's infantry."

"I'm the King's drummer," said Bertie, thumping his drum.

"Ha ha! Excellent!" wheezed Sir Harry, as his horse took him round in circles. "Well, you keep with me. We'll be guarding the King's flag."

"Can I fire the cannon?" asked Bertie.

"I don't think so!" chuckled Sir Harry. "Just stick with me. After they charge, I'm afraid we're out of the game."

"What game?" said Bertie.

"The battle, we're all killed. Didn't your dad tell you?"

"It's the battle of Bodge Hill," Dad explained. "The Roundheads win."

"Isn't that us?" said Bertie.

"No, we're the Royalists. We lose. Most of us end up dead."

Bertie frowned. "But I want to win!"

"Oh no, we can't win! Ha ha!" chuckled Sir Harry. "That wouldn't be history."

Bertie looked confused. It made no sense. What was the point of fighting a battle if you weren't trying to win? In any case, there was no way he was going to lie down and die just because it was history.

CHAPTER 4

BAM BAM! BOOM! BAM BAM!

The Royalist army set off marching up the hill. Sir Harry rode at the front with the King's flag bearer marching behind. Next came Bertie, beating his drum. Once, he dropped his drumstick and almost got trampled by a line of pikemen. At the top of the hill, he had a great view of the battlefield. The Roundhead army was drawn up in front of the tents. The King's army held the hill with the royal flag waving in the wind.

Sir Harry Crackpot made a long speech. Bertie beat his drum till he felt his arms were going to drop off. Then the two armies yelled insults at each other from a safe distance. Bertie thought it was a funny sort of battle. When were they going to get on with the fighting?

BOOM!

A cannon thundered in the distance, sending out a puff of grey smoke. *At last, this is more like it*, thought Bertie. The Roundhead army charged, waving their swords and cheering. Some of them fell over.

"This is it, men, hold your line!" yelled Sir Harry, his horse facing the wrong way.

Bertie beat his drum. He wished he had his pirate cutlass so he could fight the rotten Roundheads. Down the hill he could see Dad struggling with his pike as the enemy came into view. The two

sides met in a giant rugby scrum at the foot of the slope. Swords clashed. People cried out. Smoke filled the air. When it cleared Bertie saw a lot of the King's men were lying down, either dead or having a nap. But the enemy carried on swarming up the hill.

Bertie looked round. Sir Harry had fallen off his horse and was lying on his back. The King's flag lay forgotten in the mud. Bertie picked it up.

"No!" hissed Sir Harry urgently. "Put it down! We're all DEAD!"

"I'm not!" said Bertie. "I'm fine."

Three big Roundheads came up the hill with their swords drawn.

"You!" shouted the captain. "Hand over the flag!"

"No chance!" Bertie yelled back.

"Surrender!" ordered the captain.

"Surrender yourself!" said Bertie.

The Roundheads looked at each other. Their orders were to capture the King's flag. No one had mentioned anything about a dirty-faced drummer boy.

Bertie's dad appeared out of the smoke. He was out of breath and missing his helmet.

"Bertie, it's okay," he panted. "Let them have it! It's all part of the battle."

Bertie shook his head stubbornly. "It's the King's flag."

"I know. That's the point. We lost."

"*I* haven't lost," said Bertie. "Not yet."

The captain drew a long pistol and pointed it at him. "Bang! You're dead!" he said.

Bertie laughed. "You missed!" he cried.

The captain advanced, grimly. "Give me the flag, you little fool!"

Bertie shook his head. He raised the flagpole and brought it down on his opponent's helmet.

BASH!

"OWWW!" cried the captain, clutching his head. "Right, that's it. We're not messing about now, hand it over or else."

Bertie backed away. He was outnumbered three to one. Suddenly he had a brainwave.

"Look!" he shouted, pointing down the hill. "The King!"

The three Roundheads turned round to look. Bertie seized his chance and set off running like the wind. Down the slope he found more rotten Roundheads blocking his way. He weaved in and out of them, dodging their attempts to wrestle him to the ground.

"STOP THAT BOY!" yelled the captain. "Don't let him get away!"

But Bertie was too quick for them. In an instant he was racing across the battlefield, the royal flag streaming out in the wind. About fifty Roundheads gave chase, puffing and panting as they tried to catch up.

Dad stood with Sir Harry, watching them from the hill.

"Good Lord!" said the general. "I'm not sure it's history."

"No," said Dad, picking up his pike, "but I know someone who'll be history when I get hold of him."

Dirty Bertie

RECORD!

CHAPTER 1

Miss Boot didn't often look pleased, but today she was smiling – or at least not scowling.

There was a reason for this. Last week Swotter House School had got their picture in the paper again. Usually, this made Miss Boot green with envy – they were always winning awards or meeting some important person. But this time it had given her an idea. It was high time Pudsley Junior got their name in the paper, and she knew how.

"Can anyone tell me what this is?" she asked.

"A book!" shouted Darren.

"Don't call out please, Darren. What kind of book?"

Know-All Nick shot up his hand. "*The Bumper Book of Records*, Miss."

"I've got that book," cried Bertie. "It's fantastic!"

"Thank you, Bertie," said Miss Boot. "This is a special book all about setting records. A record is something that no one has done before."

"Like when Bertie locked Mr Grouch in the shed?" asked Darren.

"No, not like that," scowled Miss Boot. "A record is when you run faster or jump higher than anyone else. Now, I've talked to Miss Skinner and we think our school should try to set a record."

The class gasped. Bertie was so excited he almost fell off his chair. He had always wanted to set a world record – and he bet he could do it, too. Imagine it – his name in *The Bumper Book of Records*:

"The loudest burp of all time was recorded by schoolboy Bertie Burns. Bertie's burp was so loud it cracked his teacher's glasses and was heard 100 miles away in Manchester."

He would be famous. He would be interviewed on radio and TV. People would pay millions of pounds just to hear his record burp.

"So we need ideas," said Miss Boot. "What kind of record should we try to set?"

Hands waved in the air. Bertie's was the first to go up.

"Yes, Trevor," said Miss Boot.

"The highest bounce on a trampoline," said Trevor.

Miss Boot pulled a face. "Too dangerous."

"The longest tap dance," said Donna.

"Hmm, I'm not sure we've got *that* long," said Miss Boot.

Bertie's arm stretched higher. "Ooh, Miss, I know, Miss!"

"Yes, all right, Bertie," sighed Miss Boot.

"Burping!" cried Bertie.

"What?"

"Burping! I can burp really loud, ask anyone!"

Miss Boot rolled her eyes. "You cannot set a record for burping," she said.

"Why not? What about the longest burp ever?" asked Bertie. "With a bit of practice I bet I can burp for a whole minute. All I need is fizzy orange and—"

"NO, BERTIE!" snapped Miss Boot. "We are not doing anything to do with burping! Now does anyone have a sensible suggestion?"

Nisha raised her hand. "We could make a penny pyramid," she said.

Miss Boot looked interested. "A penny pyramid? Is that possible?"

Nisha nodded. "I've seen a picture. You need lots and lots of pennies."

"And where would we get them?"

"Collect them," said Nisha.

Miss Boot fingered her double chin. It might work, and it would fit in with their history work on Ancient Egypt. Better still, they were bound to get their picture in *The Pudsley Post*. It was so simple it was brilliant.

"Nisha, I think that's a splendid idea," beamed Miss Boot. "Why don't we start collecting pennies right away? Whoever collects the most will win a prize."

Bertie groaned loudly. A penny pyramid? Yawnsville! What was exciting about that? If they had to make a pyramid why not use something interesting – like slugs? Or even teachers? You could stack them on top of each other with Miss Boot at the bottom.

CHAPTER 2

That evening, Bertie explained Miss Boot's idea over supper.

"A penny pyramid?" said Dad. "What on earth is that?"

"Don't ask me," grumbled Bertie. "Miss Boot says we need to collect thousands of pennies, and whoever collects the most wins a prize."

"Have you looked in your money box?" asked Mum.

"It's empty," said Bertie. "I was sort of hoping you might help."

Dad sighed. He dug in his pocket while Mum fetched her purse. They emptied all their pennies on to the table.

"Eleven!" said Bertie, when he'd counted them. "Is that all you've got?"

"I think the word you're looking for is 'thank you'," said Dad icily.

"Oh yeah, um thank you," said Bertie. If he was going to win the prize he'd need a lot more than eleven measly pennies.

"You won't break the record anyway," sneered Suzy. "It'd have to be a huge pyramid. You'd need millions of pennies."

Bertie pushed his baked beans around the plate. Suzy was right. It was pointless. How were they ever going to collect enough pennies? It was Miss Boot's fault. Why couldn't she have picked something interesting – like the record for eating baked beans. He'd be good at that.

"How fast do you reckon I can eat these beans?" he asked.

Mum sighed. "I've no idea."

"Go on, how fast?"

"Bertie, just eat your dinner, it's not a race!"

"But say it was – say this was the World Baked Bean Eating Championship," said Bertie. "How fast do you think I could do it?"

Dad groaned. "We *don't care*!"

"Time me," said Bertie, setting down his knife and fork. Just see how long it takes. Ready… GO!"

He grabbed his plate, opened his mouth and tipped down the beans in one go.

SLURP!

"Finished!" he said, licking his lips. Tomato sauce dribbled down his chin and plopped on the table.

"EWWW! That's disgusting!" complained Suzy. "Mum, tell him!"

"That's disgusting, Bertie," said Mum. "Use your fork."

"It takes too long," said Bertie. "How quick was that?"

"We weren't timing you!" said Dad.

"About ten seconds," said Bertie. "I bet that's a world record!"

After supper, Bertie went in search of his copy of *The Bumper Book of Records.* It turned out the record for eating a tin of baked beans was under seven seconds. That was incredibly fast. It would take him longer than that to get the tin open. Bertie flicked through the pages of the book. The world's tallest man, the longest toenails, the deadliest snake, the fastest dog on a skateboard... Wait! What was that again?

"The fastest skateboarding dog is Tillman the bulldog from California, USA. Tillman skateboarded 100 metres across a car park in 19.678 seconds."

Bertie stared at the picture. A dog on a skateboard – why had he never thought of that before? It was brilliant – the greatest record ever! Much better than making a stupid pyramid out of pennies. He still had his skateboard in the shed. All he needed now was Whiffer.

CHAPTER 3

Two weeks later, the day of Pudsley Junior's world record attempt arrived. Bertie walked to school with Whiffer on a lead and his skateboard jammed into his backpack. He explained his genius idea to Darren and Eugene on the way.

"What about your mum?" asked Darren. "How did you persuade her to let you bring Whiffer to school?"

"Simple," said Bertie. "I told her that it was Bring your Pet to School day."

"And she believed you?" said Darren amazed.

Bertie nodded.

"But what if Miss Boot sees him?" said Eugene. "Dogs aren't allowed in school."

"She won't," said Bertie. "We'll smuggle him into the book cupboard before the bell goes."

"What if he barks?" objected Eugene.

"He won't. I've brought him some dog food," said Bertie. "Anyway, it's not for long, only till we go outside."

Eugene shook his head. "You're mad, Bertie! Miss Boot will go up the wall!"

"Well, I think it's a great idea," said

Darren. "Just think, we'll be famous! The world's fastest skateboarding dog!"

Eugene glanced at Whiffer doubtfully. "You think he can do it?"

"Of course he can," said Bertie. "He's been practising all week. Trust me, this will work!"

After the register, Miss Boot inspected the pennies her class had collected.

"Hands up anyone who has collected fifty or more?" she asked.

Almost every hand went up. Bertie groaned. He'd only collected twenty-four and most of those came from his gran.

"More than a hundred?" asked Miss Boot. "More than five hundred?"

Royston Rich was the only one left

with his hand up.

"Well done, Royston!" said Miss Boot. "You're the winner! How many pennies did you collect?"

Royston heaved a sack on to the table. "Two thousand," he said.

"Two thousand?"

"It was easy," said Royston smugly. "My dad went to the bank and changed a twenty pound note."

"Oh," said Miss Boot. "Well, here's your prize. Perhaps you can start your own penny collection with this." Royston stared glumly at the Peter Rabbit Money Box.

Miss Boot collected in all the pennies and divided them into buckets. She explained that they would be building the penny pyramid out in the playground. Everyone would have a chance to take part.

"And we have some special visitors," she said. "*The Pudsley Post* is sending a photographer to take our picture. Not only that, but someone is coming from *The Bumper Book of Records.*"

The class cheered excitedly.

"WOOF!" barked Whiffer in the book cupboard.

Miss Boot frowned. "What was that?"

"Um … it was me," said Bertie. "I've got a cough."

Miss Boot narrowed her eyes. "It sounded like a dog."

"Yes, it's a barking cough," said Bertie. "Woof woof!"

Miss Boot scowled. "Well, don't cough over anyone else," she said. "Right, everyone line up at the door."

Bertie breathed out. It was a close thing, but he'd got away with it.

CHAPTER 4

Outside, the penny pyramid gleamed in the sun. They had begun by laying hundreds of pennies in a square to act as the base. Then each layer had to be added carefully on top, getting smaller to create the shape of a pyramid. It was a delicate task. One slip and the whole pile would come crashing down.

They had been working for three hours in the sun. The children stood patiently waiting their turn. Miss Boot had forbidden them to run, make a noise or even whisper. *The Pudsley Post* photographer took pictures while the woman from *The Bumper Book of Records* filmed on her camcorder.

Bertie peeped round the side of the school.

"You're sure this is a good idea?" whispered Eugene.

"Stop worrying!" said Bertie.

"Yeah, it's going to be great," said Darren.

Bertie was certain Whiffer would rise to the occasion. After all, if Tillman the bulldog could ride a skateboard, any dog could do it.

"Okay, let's go," he whispered. The three of them crept out from their hiding place. Bertie kept a close eye on Miss Boot, who luckily had her back to them. He hauled Whiffer on to the skateboard and took off his lead. It took three or four attempts to get him to stay on. He kept climbing off or facing the wrong way. But at last they got him standing in position.

"Ready?" whispered Bertie. "When I say 'go' we'll push him off."

Eugene nodded and set the timer on his watch.

Whiffer didn't look thrilled to be attempting the world doggie skateboarding record. His crash helmet had slipped down over one eye and he was chewing the strap.

Miss Boot was helping Trevor to lay the next step of pennies. A few more and the pyramid would be finished. Bertie started the countdown.

"Three, two, one … GO!" he yelled.

They launched the skateboard with a mighty push. Whiffer gave a yelp as it went zooming across the playground. His ears flapped like a pair of windsocks.

"Uh oh," said Bertie.

Miss Boot had turned round – just in time to see a skateboarding dog hurtling towards her at the speed of light. For a moment she thought she must be dreaming. She stepped in front of the precious pyramid to try and prevent disaster.

"NO, STOP! STOP!" she yelled, waving her arms.

Whiffer couldn't stop, he only knew it was time to get off. He leaped into Miss Boot's arms. The skateboard zoomed on by itself.

"NOOOOOO!" yelled Miss Boot, tottering backwards.

CRASH!

Bertie hid his eyes. When he looked again Whiffer was standing on Miss Boot's chest. The class stared in horror. There were thousands of pennies scattered all over the playground.

Miss Boot pushed Whiffer off and staggered to her feet. She glared round, breathing hard. There was only one person who could have done this, and there he was trying to sneak away.

"BERTIE!" she roared. "COME HERE!"

Bertie turned round. "It wasn't my fault," he mumbled.

Miss Boot stomped towards him, purple with fury.

"LOOK!" she raged. "ALL OUR HARD WORK! WASTED! BECAUSE OF YOU!"

"I can explain," gulped Bertie.

"We might have broken the record," Miss Boot stormed. "Our picture would have been in the paper! You've ruined everything!"

"Not *everything*," mumbled Bertie. "We could always start again?"

"START AGAIN?" screamed Miss Boot. "That took us nearly FOUR HOURS!"

"Okay," said Bertie. "I've got another idea."

Miss Boot's eyes blazed. "For your sake, Bertie, it had better be good."

"It is," said Bertie. "You'll love it. All we need is a lot of fizzy orange!"

Dirty Bertie
TOOTHY!

For Ismail – another book for your collection

~ D R

For Laurie and Ed – the best kind of friends

~ A M

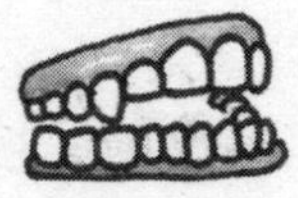

Contents

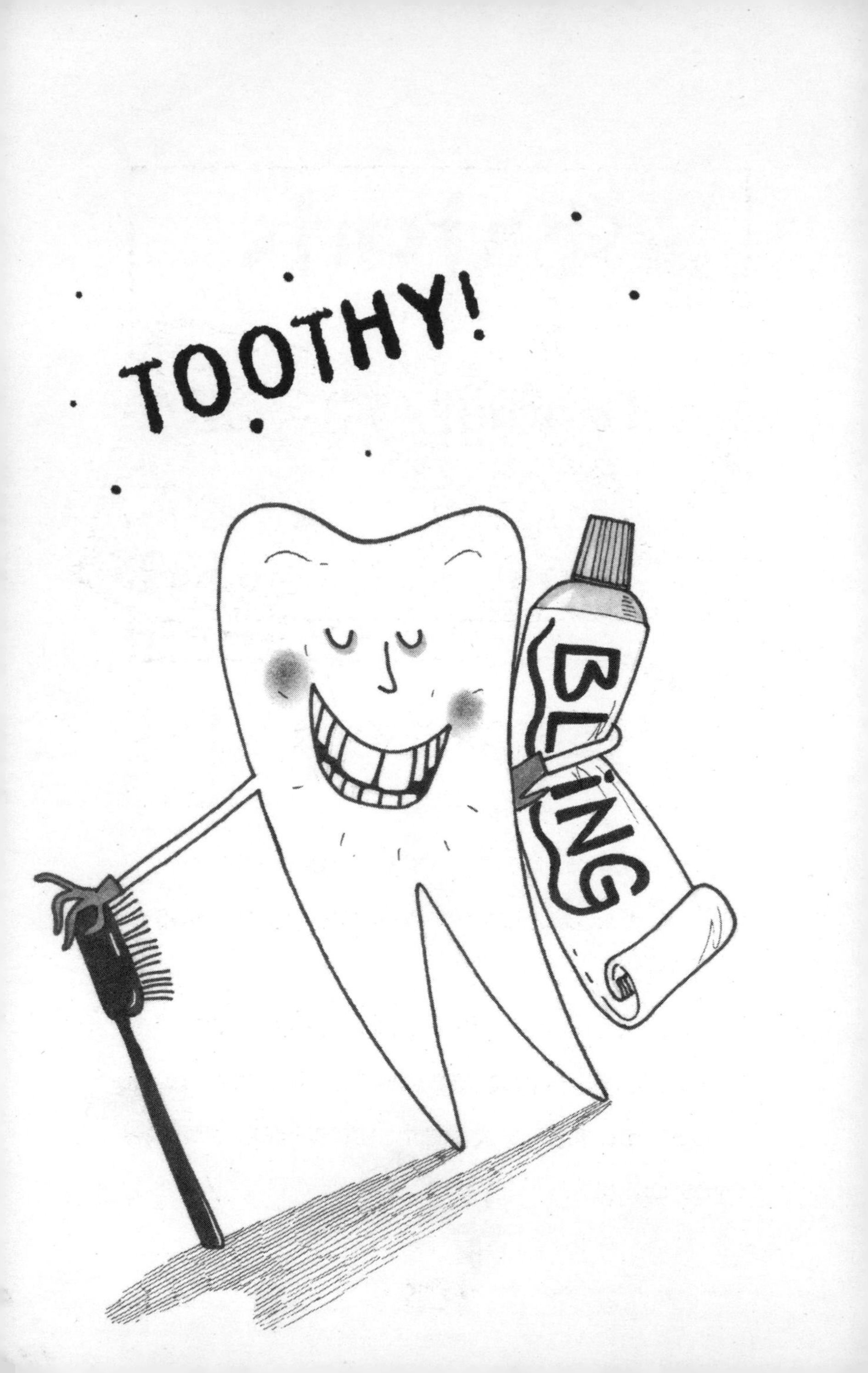
TOOTHY!
BLING

CHAPTER 1

MUNCH! CRUNCH!

Bertie was back from school and raiding the biscuit tin. Uh-oh! Mum was coming.

"Put it back, Bertie," she said. "Don't forget you've got the dentist tomorrow."

Bertie's legs suddenly felt weak. His eyes bulged.

"The dentist?"

"Yes," said Mum. "You and Suzy are due for a check-up."

"But … but I went before!" stammered Bertie.

"That was last year," said Mum.

Suzy looked up from her homework.

"I *like* going to the dentist," she said. "Mr Filling says I've got perfect teeth."

Bertie stuck out his tongue at her.

"Just 'cos you're scared," jeered Suzy.

"I'm not!" said Bertie.

"You are!" said Suzy. "Last time Mum had to drag you there."

That was a lie, thought Bertie. He'd hung on to the lamp post because he was worried they were early. Besides, it wasn't his fault that their dentist looked scary. Mr Filling had big hairy hands and mad eyes. He wore a mask over his mouth. Bertie thought he looked like a murderer.

In any case, there was nothing wrong with his teeth. None of them had fallen out, so why did he have to go? Wait a moment … didn't Mum say his check-up was tomorrow? He was saved!

"I can't go!" he said. "I've got school."

"Don't worry," said Mum. "I dropped a note in to Miss Boot this morning."

Bertie groaned.

"Anyway," said Mum, "if you clean your teeth you've nothing to worry about."

"I clean MY teeth!" boasted Suzy.

Bertie frowned. He did clean his teeth – just not every day. It saved time just to slosh water round his mouth. Now and again he used toothpaste, but mainly for drawing faces on the mirror.

He ran his tongue over his teeth. Hmm, they did feel a bit furry. What if they were crawling with toothy germs? He might need to have something done – a filling or even a tooth out! Darren said that his dentist pulled teeth out with his bare hands.

Bertie gulped. He needed to think of an excuse quickly. Wait! Mum said she'd written Miss Boot a note. So what was to stop Miss Boot writing back? Bertie rushed upstairs to find a pencil and paper.

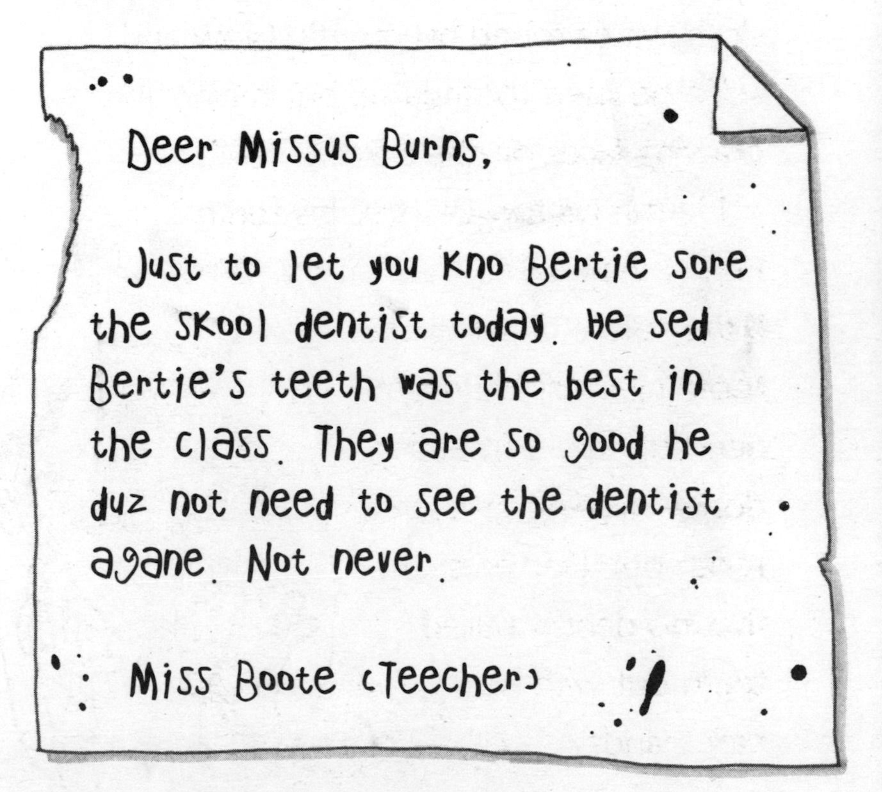
Deer Missus Burns,

Just to let you kno Bertie sore the skool dentist today. he sed Bertie's teeth was the best in the class. They are so good he duz not need to see the dentist agane. Not never.

Miss Boote (Teecher)

That should do it, thought Bertie, folding the letter in two.

He took it downstairs and waited as Mum read it through. She frowned.

"I see, and Miss Boot wrote this, did she?"

Bertie nodded. "This afternoon."

"Strange," said Mum. "Her handwriting is exactly like yours."

"Um … is it?" said Bertie.

"Yes," said Mum. "And she can't spell her own name."

She screwed up the letter and tossed it in the bin.

"Nice try, Bertie," she said. "But you are going to the dentist and that's final."

CHAPTER 2

"Ah, Bertie," breathed Mr Filling. "I've been waiting for you."

Bertie was pushed back into a chair. CLUNK! Iron rings snapped down over his wrists. He was a prisoner.

"Now, let's have a look, shall we?" cackled Mr Filling. The mask over his face slipped down, revealing two sharp fangs.

"ARGHHHHH!"

Bertie woke up in bed clutching his pillow. He opened his eyes. Thank goodness, it was only a nightmare.

What day was it today? Just a normal school day – maths, English, then... Bertie turned cold. Then THE DENTIST. HELP!

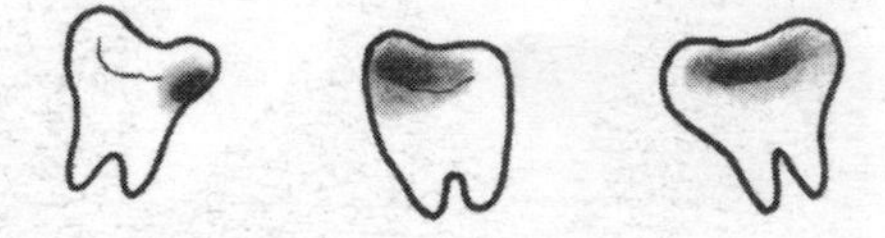

Later that day, Bertie sat in the dentist's waiting room. Suzy yawned. Mum was reading a magazine. None of the other people in the waiting room seemed nervous at all.

Bertie stared at a poster on the opposite wall. A large smiley tooth said *Brush your teeth!*

Bertie wished he was back in school – anything was better than this.

He slumped back in his chair with a groan.

"What's the matter? Scared?" said Suzy.

"Course not," said Bertie.

"You're such a baby," said Suzy.

"I'm not," scowled Bertie. "And I'm not afraid of the dentist either."

"Good," said Suzy. "Then you won't mind going first."

Bertie turned pale. Go first? Why couldn't he go last? Or better still go home?

He gripped his seat. From now on he vowed to clean his teeth ten times a day. He would even use toothpaste. He would give up sweets – apart from jelly snakes, obviously.

The dental nurse came in. "Bertie and Suzy Burns? Who's going first?" she asked.

"Bertie," said Suzy, pointing to him.

Bertie got shakily to his feet. This was it. He was a dead man.

"Good luck!" whispered Suzy. "Don't wet your pants."

"Do you want me to come with you?" asked Mum.

Bertie shook his head. He wasn't a baby.

The nurse had gone ahead. Bertie dragged himself down the corridor. Mr Filling's surgery was the last room on the left. The door was slightly open and he could hear the dentist's booming voice.

"Yes, it's a real shame," he said. "He's only seven years old."

"Is there nothing you can do?" the nurse asked.

"Afraid not. It's the kindest way, he'll have to be put to sleep."

Bertie froze. His blood ran cold. Had he imagined it? No, he'd heard it with his own ears. The dentist was planning to put him to sleep … in other words, bump him off! Bertie gulped. Hadn't he always said Mr Filling looked like a murderer? That explained why he wore gloves, so he didn't leave fingerprints!

Bertie looked around wildly. He could run back and tell his mum. But she'd never believe him. "Mr Filling – a murderer? Don't be silly, Bertie," she'd laugh. No, there was only one thing for it – he had to escape. Bertie spotted a cloakroom to his right. He slipped inside and closed the door.

3

CHAPTER 3

Bertie paced up and down, trying to stay calm. He had to get out of here before the mad murderer came for him. The nurse was obviously his evil assistant – she'd probably been hypnotized. Somehow he had to make it past the receptionist without getting caught. But how?

He looked around. Maybe he could escape through the window? But it was too high up. Or down the toilet? But what if he got stuck? His eye fell on some hats and coats hanging up beside the door. A disguise!

A minute later, Bertie slipped out of the cloakroom. He was dressed in a big grey overcoat, which dragged on the floor. He had a trilby hat pulled down over his eyes and a scarf wound round his face. He swept down the hall, trying hard not to trip on his coat-tails.

"Mr Froggat?"

Bertie halted. Did the receptionist mean him? He looked around. There was no one else about.

"Mr Froggat, if you've got a moment, please?" said the receptionist.

Bertie shuffled over to the desk, keeping his head down. The hat was too big and kept slipping over his eyes.

"We just need to book your next appointment," said the receptionist. "When would you like to come?"

Bertie wobbled his head.

"Umm num num," he mumbled.

"Sorry?" said the receptionist.

Bertie flapped his long sleeves.

"Umm num num," he repeated.

"I see," nodded the receptionist, who hadn't understood a word.

"WHAT ABOUT THE 24th, MR FROGGAT?" she shouted, as if he was deaf. "IT'S A THURSDAY!"

Bertie nodded. He didn't care what day it was, as long as he could go. The receptionist scribbled the date on a card and handed it to him.

"IS THAT ALL RIGHT?" she yelled.

"Num. Umm num," mumbled Bertie, taking the card. He hurried away. It was touch and go, but he thought he'd got away with it. All he had to do now was make it down the stairs.

"Excuse me!"

A hand tapped him on the shoulder. Argh! It was his mum!

"Have you seen a small boy?" she asked. "About this big with a runny nose?"

Bertie shook his head firmly. The hat slipped over his eyes and fell off.

Uh-oh. There was only one thing to do. Run for it!

He made a dash for the stairs, but it was no use. Mum had hold of his scarf. She reeled him in.

"And where do you think you're off to?" she said.

CHAPTER 4

Mum dragged Bertie back down the corridor to the surgery. Mr Filling turned round.

"Ah, Bertie, found you at last!" he beamed. "Trying to escape, were you? Ha ha!"

Mr Filling had a round face with eyebrows that danced around like hairy caterpillars. Bertie stared at his big hands.

"Jump up and have a seat then," he said, patting the chair. For a murderer he seemed in a pretty good mood.

Bertie looked back at Mum, who folded her arms. There was no way out. He sat down in the black leather chair. It rose up, humming as it tilted backwards. He found himself staring at pictures of dancing elephants on the ceiling.

"Okay, young man? Comfortable?" boomed Mr Filling.

Bertie nodded. His hands were starting to sweat. What was the dentist's evil plan? A deadly injection? Poisonous mouthwash? Mr Filling's masked face loomed into view. Bertie stared at his mad eyes.

"Open wide..." he said, picking up a long silver instrument.

"YEEEEEAAAARGHH!"

Bertie leaped from the chair as if he'd been shot from a catapult. He grabbed a giant toothbrush from a display.

"Keep back or I'll use it!" he cried.

Mr Filling's hairy eyebrows shot skywards. Mum advanced. Bertie bolted out of the door.

"Bertie! Get back here!" shouted Mum.

In the hallway, Bertie almost ran into the receptionist. He swerved left and burst into the waiting room. People looked up from their magazines in surprise.

"Hide me!" Bertie panted, waving his toothbrush.

Suzy rolled her eyes. "What are you on about?"

"Quick, he's coming! He's going to murder me!"

Footsteps came down the hallway. There was no time to argue. Bertie ducked behind the curtains and pulled them around him. He stood there, trying not to breathe.

Mr Filling, Mum and the dental nurse marched in.

"Where is he?" demanded Mum.

Suzy sighed. She pointed to the curtain where two dirty trainers were poking out.

Mum went over and yanked it back.

"Bertie, what are you playing at?" she cried.

"Don't let him get me!" begged Bertie.

"Who?"

"Mr Filling! He's a murderer!"

A gasp went up. Every head in the waiting room turned to look at the dentist.

Mr Filling laughed weakly. "What are you talking about? I just want to examine your teeth!"

"I heard you," said Bertie. "I heard you say you were going to put me to sleep."

Mr Filling looked baffled. Then it came back to him. "OH! I was talking about Rex," he laughed.

"Rex?"

"Yes, my dog. He's very ill and the vet says it's kindest to put him to sleep."

The heads all turned back to Bertie.

"Oh, I see … your dog," he mumbled.

Mum marched over and grabbed him. "Now, can we *please* get this over with?" she said.

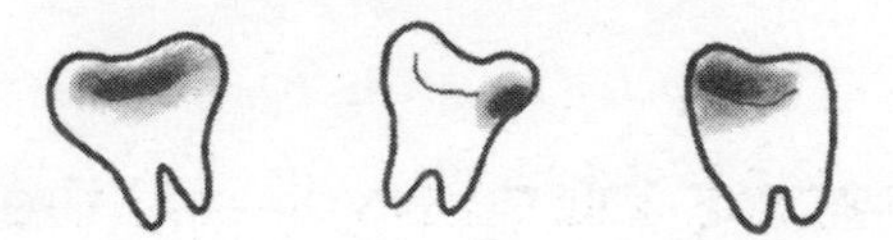

Bertie lay back in the dentist's chair while Mr Filling examined his teeth. *It wasn't my fault*, he thought. *Anyone can make a mistake.*

Mr Filling took off his mask.

"There, all done," he said.

Bertie blinked. That was it? No injections? No fillings? He hadn't felt a thing. He sat up, feeling a bit foolish. Suzy would never let him forget this. Wait till the story got round school – Bertie hiding from the dentist. He'd never hear the last of it. "Scaredy-cat! Cowardy custard!" they'd call after him.

"Your teeth are fine," said Mr Filling. "Just don't forget to clean them."

Bertie climbed down from the chair.

"I'm sorry about … you know … before," he mumbled.

Mr Filling laughed.

"Oh, don't worry, I'm used to nervous patients. Your sister used to be the worst."

"Suzy?" said Bertie. This was news to him.

"Oh, yes, she used to scream if I came near her," smiled Mr Filling. "I had to give her Mr Teddikins to cuddle." He pointed to a large, goggle-eyed teddy bear in the corner.

Bertie smiled to himself. Mr Teddikins, eh? Wait till the next time Suzy called him a cry baby. She was never going to tease him again!

ZOOM!

CHAPTER 1

Mum burst into the kitchen excitedly.

"The holiday's booked!" she said. "And we're flying out!"

Suzy whooped. Dad groaned. Bertie almost fainted. Had he heard right? Was he dreaming?

"Flying?" he said.

"That's right," said Mum.

"On a plane?"

"Of course on a plane, how else?"

"WAHOO!"

Bertie had never flown in his life. Loads of his friends had been on planes. Eugene said it was amazing. They showed films and brought you free drinks! Royston Rich claimed he'd been up in his dad's private jet. But Bertie had never even been to an airport. Whenever they'd talked about flying, Dad always found an excuse.

"Is Whiffer coming?" asked Bertie.

"Dogs aren't allowed on planes," said Dad. "Now, on the car ferry—"

"Don't start," sighed Mum wearily. "We agreed."

"Where are we sitting? Can I sit next to the pilot?" asked Bertie.

"No," said Dad firmly. "You sit where you're told."

Bertie didn't think Dad sounded that thrilled to be going on a plane. But *he* was. Wait till he told Darren and Eugene!

"When do we go?" asked Suzy.

"In half term. That's three weeks," said Mum.

THREE WHOLE WEEKS! That was ages! Bertie didn't think he could wait that long.

"EEEEOWWW!" he cried, taking off

and zooming round the kitchen. He swooped down at supersonic speed, then trod in Whiffer's bowl and skidded…

"Yarghhh!"

CRASH!

"BERTIE!" yelled Dad.

Bertie scrambled to his feet. Honestly, some people were so touchy!

CHAPTER 2

Three weeks later, the great day finally dawned. Bertie was so excited he'd been dressed since 5 a.m. His bag had been packed for weeks. He had everything he needed for the flight: sweets, comics, his Jumbo Jet Sticker Book and more sweets, in case he ran out.

At the airport, Dad loaded the cases

on to a trolley and they went inside. Bertie hurried past the shops and cafés.

"Can we get on the plane now?" he said. "I want to get a good seat."

Suzy rolled her eyes. "It's not going for hours! We need tickets."

"Yes," said Mum. "First we have to check in and get our boarding passes."

The queue at the desk tailed back for about a mile. Bertie stared in horror.

"What? We've got to wait behind all these people?" he groaned.

"I'm afraid so," sighed Mum.

"But we'll miss the plane! Why can't we go to that desk?"

He pointed to the next one, where no one was waiting.

"That's not our airline," said Dad. "We're flying with Cheapy Jet."

They joined the queue and waited as it shuffled forward at a snail's pace.

"Can I push the trolley?" begged Bertie.

"No," said Dad.

"But Suzy's had her turn!"

"Don't argue!" snapped Dad.

Bertie let go of the trolley. Dad had been in a bad mood since breakfast.

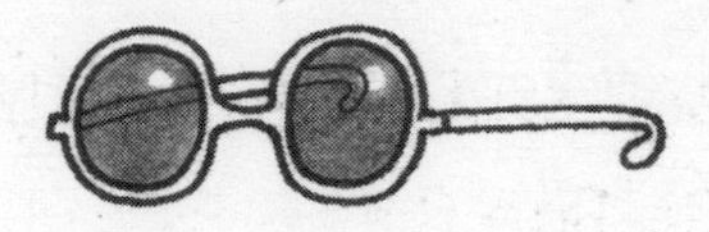

After half an hour they reached the desk and got their boarding passes. Next they queued at Passport Control. Then they joined the end of the snaking line at security. Finally, they had to wait an hour at the gate because their flight was delayed. Bertie couldn't believe catching a plane took so long. With buses you just got on!

At long last it was time to board. Bertie hurtled up the steps.

"Bags I sit by the window!" he cried, racing down the gangway. There were three seats to a row. Bertie plonked himself down by the window and took out his sweets.

"Who's sitting with Bertie?" asked Dad.

"You can," said Mum, quickly. "I'll sit behind with Suzy."

Dad sank into his seat. Bertie was staring out of the window, sucking a fruity chew. At last, this was it – he was actually going to fly!

"Aren't you excited?" he asked, bouncing up and down.

"Not really," said Dad. "Fasten your seatbelt."

Bertie wasn't listening. He reached up to a switch above him.

"What's this?"

CLICK! A light came on.

"A reading light," said Dad. "Leave it alone."

"And what does this one do?" asked Bertie, fiddling with a catch on the seat in front.

CLONK! A table flopped down, knocking his sweets out of his hand. Bertie scrambled on the floor to find them. Dad shut his eyes. Three hours on a plane with Bertie! He didn't know if his nerves could stand it.

None of the other passengers seemed to want the seat next to them. Eventually, a tall, elderly man sat down. He had big pink ears and a grumpy expression.

Bertie leaned over. "It's my first time on a plane," he said.

"Really," said Big Ears.

"Yes. Is it yours?"

"No," said Big Ears. He shook open his newspaper and hid behind it.

"Welcome aboard this Cheapy Jet Flight 647," said a voice over the tannoy. "Please listen carefully while we go through the safety procedures..."

Bertie leaned forward to watch as the flight attendants waved their arms.

"There are three emergency exits: here, here and here..."

"What's an emergency exit?" Bertie whispered.

"It's the way out in an emergency," said Dad.

"What sort of emergency?"

Dad sighed. "It doesn't matter."

"You mean like if one of the wings drops off?" asked Bertie.

"Hopefully that won't happen," replied Dad, loosening his collar.

The voice went on. "You'll find a life jacket under your seat..."

"Have I got one?" Bertie asked.

"Yes," said Dad.

"Can I put it on now?"

"No!" groaned Dad. "It's only for ... well, if we came down in the sea."

"In the sea? WOW!" said Bertie. "You mean like if we crash-land because the plane's on fire..."

"Bertie, *please*!" moaned Dad.

"I was only asking," said Bertie.

The plane shook as the engines rumbled into life. Dad gripped the arms of his seat.

"This is it. We're going!" cried Bertie.

Dad closed his eyes. He seemed to be praying. The plane bumped out towards the runway. It swung sharp left then began to pick up speed. Dad shrank back in his seat. Bertie had his nose glued to the window, so he didn't miss a thing.

"We're up!" he yelled. "Wahoo! Look, you can see the airport. And the cars! They're tiny, look!"

Dad moaned. "I don't want to look!"

"Why not?" asked Bertie.

"Because I hate flying, okay? It makes me nervous."

Bertie frowned. How could anyone hate flying? It was brilliant – even better than going on a roller coaster.

CHAPTER 3

Bertie stared out of the window at the vast blue sky. They'd been flying for ages now. Dad was listening to music on his headphones. Bertie had eaten all his sweets. He was bored. A flight attendant came past pushing the drinks trolley. Her badge said "Tina".

Bertie nudged Dad.

"Can I have some crisps?"

"What? No!"

"How about a Coke?"

"You're not having anything," said Dad. "Read your comic."

Bertie sighed. He had already read his comic *and* done his sticker book. It turned out they weren't even showing a film. No wonder the airline was called Cheapy Jet! He found a button on his armrest that he hadn't tried yet.

CLUNK!

His seat suddenly flipped backwards.

"OWW!" wailed Suzy. "Mum!"

"Bertie!" sighed Mum.

"It wasn't my fault," said Bertie. "How was I to know it did that?"

"Just sit still and leave things alone," said Mum.

Bertie tilted his seat back up. He'd been sitting still for ages. His bottom ached. He poked Dad again.

"What now?" said Dad, removing his headphones.

"I need the toilet!" said Bertie.

Dad sighed. "It's at the front."

Bertie clambered past Dad and Big Ears and made his way down the aisle. He had to pass Tina, who was heading back with the drinks trolley. Bertie eyed the bags of crisps hungrily.

"Can I help you?" asked Tina.

"I need the toilet," said Bertie.

"It's occupied at the moment. You can wait outside," said Tina.

She disappeared behind a grey curtain with the trolley. Bertie stood tapping his feet. Whoever was in the toilet was taking ages! He wondered what happened when you flushed the loo on a plane. Did everything shoot out into the sky? Tina came out again and went down the aisle with the trolley.

Bertie stared at the curtain. Maybe that was where the drinks and snacks were kept – the ones nobody wanted? It seemed a pity to waste them. No one was about, so he slipped through the curtain. He found himself looking at a wall of metal cases. Bertie tried to open one, but it wouldn't budge. Then he spotted something else – a panel of switches and buttons on the wall. At the top – just in reach – was a large red button.

Bertie had been told a million times not to touch things, especially things like worms and snails. But buttons were different. Bertie loved pressing them because he wanted to know what they did. Maybe this one fired the booster rockets? Or set the plane to warp speed? Bertie reached out a finger and pressed…

WOOP! WOOP! WOOP! WOOP!

Yikes! A red light began to flash.

Bertie ducked back through the curtain just as Tina came hurrying up the gangway.

"I'm sorry, you'll have to return to your seat," she said.

"But I still need the toilet," said Bertie.

"The seatbelt sign is on. Everyone must take their seats," said Tina firmly.

Bertie headed back, with the alarm ringing in his ears. People were looking round. This was not good. What if they found out it was him who set off the alarm? Maybe he'd be arrested. Or thrown out of the emergency exit!

CHAPTER 4

Bertie sank back in his seat.

"What's going on?" asked Dad.

"I don't know!" said Bertie. "I only went to the toilet."

Dad clutched at the arm of his seat.

"What's that alarm? Is something wrong?" he worried.

"It's probably just a mistake," said Bertie.

"A fire alarm or something."

"A *FIRE ALARM*?" cried Dad.

"Did you say *fire*?" shouted Big Ears.

Bertie wished he'd never mentioned it.

"I didn't say there was…" he began.

But it was too late. The rumour was spreading from one row to the next.

"A fire? Where?"

"I don't know."

"Someone said they smelled smoke!"

"It's one of the engines!"

"Good grief! Are we going to be all right?"

Dad had gone white. He was breathing heavily. Big Ears was arguing loudly with the man in front. A baby started wailing. Bertie sunk down in his seat. *Help!* he thought. *All I did was press one little button!*

A voice on the tannoy rang out. "If I can have your attention! Everyone *please* stay in their seats. There is no reason to panic."

Flight attendants hurried to and fro, trying to calm everyone down.

Tina came past.

"What's that alarm?" Big Ears demanded.

"Nothing to worry about, sir," said Tina.

"Are we on fire?"

"No, of course not," said Tina.

WOOP! WOOP! WOO—

The alarm suddenly stopped. Silence fell. It was broken by a new voice over the tannoy.

"Captain Rogers here. Awfully sorry about that. It seems someone set off an alarm by mistake. Anyway, no harm done. Please remain seated while the cabin crew come round and serve refreshments."

Everyone breathed a huge sigh of relief. Big Ears went back to his paper, muttering to himself. Dad slumped back in his seat, exhausted. Bertie puffed out his cheeks.

Tina appeared again, pushing the drinks trolley.

"Any drinks? Tea, coffee, juice?" she asked.

"Tea," said Big Ears. "And maybe you

can tell me exactly how this alarm went off?"

"We don't know, sir," said Tina. "It could have been a passenger."

"Where was it?"

Tina pointed. "In the serving area, past the toilet."

Dad frowned. A worrying thought crossed his mind. Where was Bertie when the alarm went off? He turned to him.

"Did you have anything to do with this?"

"M-me?" gulped Bertie.

"Yes, you. Did you set off the alarm?"

"No!" said Bertie. "I never touched it!"

"Touched what?" said Dad.

"You know … the thing … the red button."

Dad narrowed his eyes. "How do you know it's a red button?" he said.

"Um…" said Bertie.

Nobody spoke much to Bertie for the rest of the flight. Dad kept his headphones on. Mum had her nose in her book. Now and again, other passengers turned round to glare in Bertie's direction.

At last, the plane came in to land. Dad grabbed their bags and they hurried off.

At the bottom of the steps a young man was waiting. He handed them a card.

"Would you like to fill in our Cheapy Jet survey?" he asked. "You could win a free flight for all the family."

"A free flight?" said Dad.

"Fantastic!" cried Bertie.

Mum and Dad looked down at him.

"No, thanks," said Dad, handing back the card. "We are *never* going on a plane again!" "

HOT!

CHAPTER 1

It was hot. Scorching hot. Sitting at the back of the class, Bertie felt he was going to melt. It was ages till afternoon break. His head flopped on to his desk. He was certain it must be 1000 degrees. There ought to be a law against going to school in this heat.

It was all right for teachers, he thought

bitterly. Miss Boot had a fan on her desk to keep her cool. The rest of them had to roast. Eugene's cheeks had gone bright pink. Darren's hair was sticking up like a paintbrush. Only Know-All Nick looked as pale and neat as ever.

Bertie moaned. "I'm dying of thirst!"

"Me, too," said Darren. "Ask Miss Boot if we can get a drink."

"You ask her," replied Bertie.

Darren raised his hand.

"Miss, please may I go to the toilet?"

"Certainly not. Wait till break time," snapped Miss Boot.

Darren squirmed in his seat.

"Pleeeeease! I've been holding on since lunchtime!"

Miss Boot rolled her eyes.

"Oh, very well."

Darren got up, giving Bertie a wink as he left the class. There was a drinking fountain by the boys' toilets. Bertie watched him go and stuck up his hand.

"Miss..."

"No, you can't," snapped Miss Boot.

"But Miss, I..."

"No means NO!" thundered Miss Boot.

Bertie's shoulders slumped. It was so unfair! How come Darren got to go and he didn't? He glanced up at the clock. He'd never last till break. He was actually *dying* of thirst. Soon he'd be nothing but clothes in a puddle of sweat.

DING-A-DING! DING-A-DING!

Bertie sat up. He knew that sound. It was Mr Frosty's ice-cream van! The van tootled down the road, playing its merry tune, and parked near the school gates. Bertie stared out of the window. What he would give now for a juicy Cola-Cooler lolly! Or an extra-large cone with soft ice cream…

"BERTIE!"

Miss Boot was standing over him.

"Yes, Miss?"

"Get on with your work. You haven't written two words."

Bertie sighed. It was cruelty. He *needed* an ice cream. Besides, ice cream was good for you. It contained healthy stuff like um … cream. If Miss Boot wasn't such a meanie, she would go and buy him one.

CHAPTER 2

At break time Bertie and his friends stood staring out through the fence. They watched the nursery children come out and get ice creams.

This is torture, thought Bertie. The van was parked ten metres up the road, but it might as well have been a million miles. School was just like prison.

The gates were locked and the teachers were on patrol at all times.

"There *must* be a way," said Bertie.

"Face it," said Eugene. "It's impossible."

Darren nodded. "Forget it."

Bertie flopped against the fence. All he wanted was one teeny-weeny ice cream (with a chocolate flake). Was that too much to ask? If he closed his eyes, he could almost taste it. Smooth, silky ice cream slipping down his throat.

He opened his eyes and stared at the fence. There had to be a way out somewhere… Hang on, what was that? A little further along, the wire fence was bent back. It left a tiny gap underneath, big enough for a cat or a small person to crawl through. They could escape! There was just one problem – Miss Boot was on playground duty. If she spotted them, she'd swoop down like a fire-breathing dragon.

Bertie racked his brains. They needed some way to distract her. But what? Eugene tap-dancing? Know-All Nick yelling that his pants were on fire? What would get Miss Boot's *full* attention? Bertie smiled. He knew just the thing.

Miss Boot sat on a bench in the shade, fanning herself with her sun hat. Darren wandered over.

"Miss," he said. "What do rats look like?"

Miss Boot frowned. "Rats?" she said. "They're like mice, only bigger and dirtier. Why?"

"Oh, nothing. It's just I thought I saw one," said Darren.

Miss Boot turned pale. *Rats? In the school?* If there was one thing she hated it was rats. Filthy, horrible vermin!

"Where?" she said.

"Over there," said Darren, pointing to the rubbish bins.

Miss Boot followed him over. She was certain Darren had imagined it. All the same, she didn't want to get too close, just in case. If there was a rat, it might run over her foot – or even up her leg. She shuddered at the thought.

"Where was it?" she demanded.

"Just there, Miss, by the bin," said Darren. "A great big rat with blood-red eyes and pointy teeth."

Miss Boot went a bit closer. She bent down to look.

THUMP!

Suddenly, one of the bins jumped.

"ARRRRRGHH!" screamed Miss Boot, leaping back. If that was a rat, it was a monster. A king rat!

"I'll er … I'll fetch Mr Grouch," she gulped. "Rats are his job, really. Keep away from there, Darren."

She hurried off to find the caretaker.

As soon as she was gone, Eugene popped up from behind the bin.

"Did it work?" he asked.

"Like a dream," said Darren. He hurried over to Bertie by the fence.

"All clear?" said Bertie.

"Yes, but you'd better be quick," said Darren, holding up the fence.

They didn't have long. Miss Boot would be back any minute with Mr Grouch. Bertie looked around. No one was watching. He got down and squeezed through the small hole. Now to grab the ice creams and make it back before anyone saw him.

CHAPTER 3

Bertie waited, hopping from foot to foot. There were two other people in the queue and they were taking ages. At any moment he expected to hear Miss Boot screeching his name. At last he reached the front.

"Three large cones, please," he said. "With sprinkles and a chocolate flake."

He watched the smooth, soft ice cream ooze from the nozzle.

"Three pounds," said the ice-cream man.

Bertie handed over the money they'd scraped together and grabbed the cones. He'd been dreaming of this moment all day. He lifted one of the ice creams to his mouth…

DRRRRING!

Bertie looked up. No way! Surely that couldn't be the bell already?

But the playground was starting to empty. His class were lining up under the stern eye of Miss Boot. Bertie quickly ducked out of sight behind a tree.

Darren stood in line with Eugene. He glanced back towards the fence. There was no sign of Bertie. What was he playing at? A hand tapped him on the shoulder. He turned round to see Know-All Nick's smug face.

"Where's Bertie?" Nick asked.

"How should I know?" shrugged Darren. "He's here somewhere."

Nick looked around. "Really? I don't see him. Shall I tell Miss Boot?"

"Mind your own business," said Darren.

"No talking!" shouted Miss Boot. They trooped inside.

Bertie came out from behind the tree and stared at the empty playground.

Help! Now what? He couldn't crawl under the fence without Darren to hold it up. And anyway, he had his hands full of ice creams. This was terrible! He'd escaped, but now he couldn't get back in!

Ice cream dripped down his fingers. How could he give Darren and Eugene their cornets now? But if he hung on to them, they'd only melt! It seemed a pity to let them go to waste. Bertie licked his own ice cream, then the other two.

All his class would be sitting down now. And Miss Boot would be sure to notice his empty chair. Sooner or later she'd worm the truth out of Darren and Eugene. Then a search party would be sent out with sniffer dogs. If they found him, he was in BIG trouble. Miss Boot would move him away from his friends. He'd have to sit at the front – probably next to a GIRL! Bertie felt ill at the thought. Somehow he had to get back into school.

As he stood there, a lorry drew up

and the driver jumped out.

"S'cuse me, son, is this Pudsley Junior?" he asked.

Bertie nodded.

"Thanks," said the driver. He looked at Bertie and frowned. "Shouldn't you be in school?"

"Er no," said Bertie. "I'm um … off sick."

"Right. So you're buying ice creams?"

"Oh no, they're not mine, I'm just looking after them," explained Bertie.

"Course you are," smiled the driver. He went back to the lorry, laughing to himself. Another man got out, and together they unloaded two large boxes from the back of the lorry. Bertie watched, licking his three cones.

The driver went to the gates and spoke into the intercom. A moment later, the gates began to open and the men carried one of the boxes inside. *This is it*, thought Bertie, *my chance to get in*! But wait – what about Mrs Duff, the school secretary? No one got past her eagle eyes. There had to be another way. Bertie looked at the remaining cardboard box sitting beside the lorry. Quickly, he opened it up. Inside were some flat bits of wood and a bag of screws. Maybe there was just enough room? Clutching his ice cream cones, Bertie climbed into the box.

CHAPTER 4

A few minutes later, the two men returned.

"This one as well? What's in them?" said the driver's mate.

"How should I know? Just pick it up."

Bertie heard a lot of grunting and felt the box lift off the ground.

"It weighs a ton! They got a dead

body in here?"

Inside the box, Bertie hardly dared to breathe. All he had to do was wait till the box was set down. Then he could slip out quietly and sneak back to his class. With a bit of luck, Miss Boot hadn't even noticed he was missing. He licked one of the cones – no point in saving them now...

Back in class, Darren and Eugene were starting to worry.

"Where is he?" hissed Eugene.

"Search me," said Darren. "Where are our ice creams?"

"Maybe he can't get back under the fence," worried Eugene. He looked round and caught Know-All Nick's eye.

Trust that nosy creep to be snooping around, thought Eugene. *How much does he know? Did he see Bertie escape? Uh-oh, he's putting his hand up.*

"Miss Boot," said Nick. "Where's Bertie?"

Miss Boot looked up. "Bertie?" She stared at the empty chair where Bertie normally sat.

"Where *is* Bertie?" she demanded.

"I don't know," said Nick slyly. "I haven't seen him since break. Maybe he's run away!"

Miss Boot frowned. "Darren? Do you know?"

Darren's mind was a blank. "Oh he's er ... he's..."

"...He's gone to wash his hands," said Eugene, quickly.

"Why?" said Miss Boot.

"They were dirty," said Eugene.

Miss Boot narrowed her eyes. Bertie's hands were always dirty, but he'd never felt the need to wash them before. Besides, it was ten minutes since break. Where had the dratted boy got to this time? Knowing Bertie, he was somewhere he shouldn't be.

"Give him one minute, then go and fetch him," she ordered.

Just then there was a knock at the door.

Two men in blue overalls shuffled in, carrying a large box.

"Delivery," panted one of them. "Where do you want it?"

"Put it over there," said Miss Boot.

She had been waiting for the new TV cabinet for weeks. But she could deal with that later, once she'd found Bertie.

Inside the box, Bertie was getting cramp. His knees were squashed in his face. Maybe it was safe to get out now? He peeped through a tiny hole in the box. He could see a thick pair of woollen tights. Yikes! He knew those tree-trunk legs – they were Miss Boot's! He was back in his own classroom.

There was nothing for it but to sit tight and wait till everyone went home. At least he still had one cone left.

CRUNCH!

Know-All Nick looked up. What was that noise? It had come from the box. Should he tell Miss Boot? He shot up his hand.

"Miss!"

"Not now, Nicholas," sighed Miss Boot.

"But Miss, I think there's something in the box," said Nick.

"Yes, it's a TV cabinet," said Miss Boot.

"But I heard it, Miss, it made a noise!"

Miss Boot frowned. First it was rats by the bins, now strange noises – there was something funny going on. She approached the cardboard box. Eugene and Darren looked at each other. Surely it couldn't be…?

Miss Boot ripped opened the flaps. She gasped.

A face rose slowly from the box. Bertie had ice cream round his mouth. Large blobs had dripped all down his shirt.

"The greedy pig!" gasped Darren. "He ate them all!"

"BERTIE!" boomed Miss Boot. "What *are* you doing in there?"

"Um … well…" said Bertie.

Miss Boot pulled him out by the arm. "Wait, what is that on your face?" she said.

"Have you been eating *ice cream*?"

Bertie swallowed. He brought out a messy blob from his pocket.

"Chocolate flake?" he said.

Dirty Bertie
DINOSAUR!

For Merv ~ D R

For Spike and Rudy ~ A M

Contents

DINOSAUR!

CHAPTER 1

"Whiffer, here boy. HERE!" cried Bertie.

Whiffer streaked across the park and vanished into the trees. Bertie rolled his eyes. It was always like this. As soon as Whiffer escaped his lead he zoomed off like a hairy torpedo.

Luckily, Darren and Eugene had come to help.

"Where's he gone?" groaned Darren.

"No idea," said Bertie. "He's probably seen a squirrel or something."

They found Whiffer under the trees, wagging his tail excitedly. He was scrabbling at something in the dirt.

Bertie bent down to pick it up. "Look at this!" he cried.

"What is it? Some sort of bone?" asked Darren.

Bertie rubbed off some of the dirt. "It's a tooth," he said.

"Pretty large one," said Eugene. "Maybe it's a wolf's fang?"

Bertie shook his head. "Too big," he said. "That's a *dinosaur* tooth!"

"No way!" said Darren.

"How do you know?" asked Eugene.

"I've seen pictures," said Bertie. "In my *Dangerous Book of Dinosaurs*."

"Miss Boot says dinosaurs are extinct," said Eugene. "That tooth could be millions of years old."

Bertie frowned. "It doesn't look millions of years old."

"It must be," said Darren. "Unless a dinosaur was round here recently."

Bertie looked up. He had always dreamed of seeing an actual dinosaur – a Stegosaurus or maybe a Tyrannosaurus rex.

"Maybe they're not all extinct," he said.

"What!" Darren frowned. "You mean there's one living in the park?"

"I'm not saying there is," said Bertie. "But if I was a dinosaur, this is exactly the kind of place I'd hide."

They looked around uneasily. Suddenly the park didn't seem such a safe place.

"Hey, look at this!" cried Eugene. He pointed to some deep scratches on the bark of a tree.

"A dog could have done that," said Darren.

"Yes – or something much bigger," said Bertie.

Eugene shivered. "Um … maybe we should get back," he said.

"Good idea," said Darren. "Before it gets dark."

Bertie put Whiffer on his lead. As they hurried out of the trees they bumped into Angela Nicely. Bertie groaned.

Angela lived next door and was always trailing around after him. Only last week she'd turned up at his house asking if he wanted to play.

"I knew it was you!" she trilled. "What are you doing?"

"Nothing," said Bertie, hiding the dinosaur tooth behind his back.

"I've been watching," said Angela. "You found something."

"Only some old ants' nest," said Bertie quickly.

Angela shook her head. "Liar," she said. "Was it treasure?"

"No," said Bertie.

"I bet it was," said Angela.

"It wasn't," said Bertie. "Oh look, I think your friends want you."

Angela glanced back at the swings where Maisie and Laura were waiting. Bertie took the chance to slip the tooth into his pocket – but Angela saw.

"What's that?" she demanded.

"What?"

"That, in your pocket. Show me!"

"It's nothing," said Bertie. "Anyway we've got to get back."

He hurried after Darren and Eugene

Angela watched them go. Bertie was definitely hiding something. It was some sort of secret. Well, she would find out – if there was one thing she loved, it was a secret.

CHAPTER 2

On Saturday morning, Bertie waited excitedly for Darren and Eugene to arrive. He was determined to prove there really was a dinosaur living in the park. And if there was, he wanted to be the one to catch it. Imagine capturing the last dinosaur on earth! They'd be rich! They'd be famous! He could charge people ten pounds a go to ride on its back!

They trooped down to the park, carrying spades. Eugene had brought his junior binoculars and Darren had some netting slung over his shoulder.

"Even if there is a dinosaur," said Darren, "I don't see how we're going to catch it."

"By making a trap," said Bertie. "We'll dig a hole and cover it over with branches and stuff so no one can see it. When the dinosaur comes along, it'll fall right in."

Eugene looked doubtful. "It'll need to be a big hole," he said. "Dinosaurs are massive."

"We'll make it big," said Bertie. "Really big."

They crossed the park and reached

the trees where they'd found the tooth.

Bertie pointed to a muddy clearing. "We'll dig here," he said.

"What if the park keeper comes?" Eugene asked anxiously.

"He won't," said Bertie. "*Anyway*, he ought to be grateful. If there is a dinosaur, someone should catch it before anyone gets eaten!"

Eugene looked around nervously. Secretly he hoped the dinosaur didn't exist. Maybe the tooth was really just a stone?

They got on with the digging. It took a long time, but at last they'd dug a big hole deep enough to stand in.

Bertie jumped in to test it. "That'll do," he panted, as Darren heaved him out. "Let's cover it up."

They laid branches across the top and covered them with leaves and clods of earth. Bertie stood back to admire their work. No one would ever know the trap was there. And anyway, he was pretty sure that dinosaurs were short sighted.

"What about sticks?" said Darren. "In case it puts up a fight."

They each found a stick then hid in some bushes to wait.

Ten minutes passed. Eugene scanned the trees with his binoculars. Darren complained his leg had gone to sleep.

Suddenly Bertie sat up. "Listen!" he hissed. "Something's coming!"

They got ready to jump out. Eugene's heart thumped. He hoped it was a Diplodocus because they were vegetarian.

The bushes rustled. Then something stepped into the clearing.

"BERTIE! WHERE ARE YOU?"

Bertie groaned. Not Angela again!

"What do *you* want?" he cried, coming out from the bushes.

"Found you!" cried Angela triumphantly. "Are we playing pirates?"

"No!" said Bertie. "And don't come any closer or you'll fall in our trap."

Angela noticed the covered hole and crouched down to inspect it.

"Oooh! Did you make it?" she asked.

"Course we made it," said Bertie. "And now you've seen it, you can go."

"I'm not going till you tell me what it's for," said Angela stubbornly.

Bertie and his friends looked at each other. They knew that threatening Angela with spiders or slugs had no effect.

Eugene sighed. "We're hunting a dinosaur, okay?"

Bertie rolled his eyes. Now they'd never get rid of her.

"A *dinosaur*?" cried Angela.

"Not so loud!" said Bertie. "We found one of its teeth so it'll probably come back. Then we can catch it."

Angela shook her head. "You won't," she said matter-of-factly. "Not here."

"Yeah? How would you know?" demanded Darren.

"I've seen it," said Angela.

"Seen it?" said Bertie. "You've seen an *actual real* dinosaur?"

"Yes!" said Angela, beaming at them.

"She's making it up!" snorted Darren.

"No, I'm not," said Angela. "I'll show you if you like. It's not far."

CHAPTER 3

They followed Angela out of the park and a little way down Bertie's road. She stopped outside number twelve.

"Here?" said Bertie.

Mr Monk lived at number twelve and he was Bertie's least favourite person. Mr Monk said Bertie's parents should keep him locked up.

Only last week he'd gone on and on about riding bikes on the pavement. And he was always grumbling about dog's muck on the street as if Whiffer was responsible for all of it. He'd written to the local paper to complain. Twice.

They all crouched down behind the hedge.

"There!" said Angela, pointing to the top window. "See it?"

They raised their heads and stared in amazement. There, peering out from behind the curtain, was a real dinosaur! It had green scales, jagged teeth and hungry eyes that watched the street.

"A Tyrannosaurus!" gasped Bertie.

"I told you," said Angela triumphantly.

"But what's it doing there?" asked Eugene.

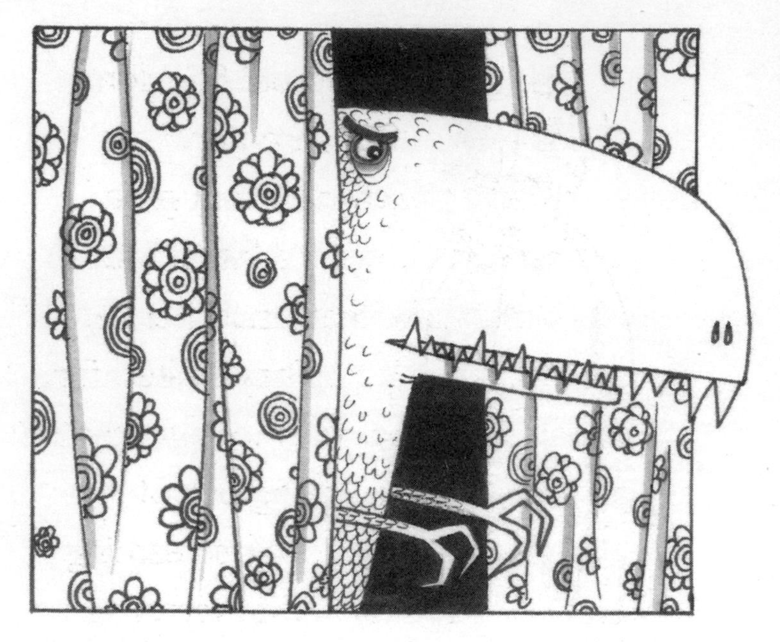

"Maybe it broke in," said Bertie. "Maybe it got hungry and ate Mr Monk."

"I don't think so," said Darren. "Here he comes."

They ducked down behind the hedge just in time. Mr Monk came marching down the street, carrying a bag. He turned into his drive and unlocked the door to go in.

"Uh oh! Shouldn't we warn him?" whispered Eugene.

"It's a bit late for that," said Bertie.

They waited for Mr Monk to come flying out of the door screaming with terror. Minutes passed – nothing happened.

Bertie frowned. "You know what I think?" he said. "He's keeping the dinosaur as a pet. I bet he's training it to attack children – especially if they're riding bikes on the pavement."

Angela tugged at his arm. "What shall we do?"

"Capture it," said Bertie. "We've still

got our sticks and the net."

He didn't see why Mr Monk should keep the dinosaur. After all, *he* was the one who'd found the tooth. And besides, it was cruel to keep a dinosaur indoors.

Eugene gulped. "But shouldn't we tell the police?"

Bertie snorted. "The police? You think they'll believe us?"

The others shook their heads. It did sound hard to believe – a Tyrannosaurus living on Fleaman Drive.

"It's up to us," said Bertie. "We've got to get in without old Monk seeing us. Angela, you'll have to keep him busy at the door."

CHAPTER 4

DING DONG!

Angela reached up and rang Mr Monk's doorbell. She glanced back at the others and winked with both eyes. That was the signal.

"Quick! Let's go!" said Bertie.

They slipped through the side gate and crept round the back of the house.

Mr Monk's back door was open.

Bertie grasped his stick. He couldn't decide which would be scarier – facing a Tyrannosaurus or a hopping mad Mr Monk.

"What if it eats one of us?" whispered Eugene, trembling.

"Don't worry, we'll catch it in the net," said Bertie. "If it grabs you, use your stick."

Darren and Eugene nodded. They followed Bertie in through the back door and tiptoed into the hall.

Mr Monk was outside his front door, hunting for whoever had rung his bell.

They sneaked up the stairs and paused – all was quiet on the landing. Bertie tiptoed over and peeped through the crack of a door.

"It's in there all right," he whispered.

"Couldn't we come back when it's asleep?" pleaded Eugene.

Bertie shook his head. It was now or never. "I'll count to three, then we charge," he said. "One ... two ... THREE!"

They burst into the room, yelling like savages. The dinosaur was looking out of the window with its back to them. They could see its long tail and scaly green head. Darren ran and threw the net. Then they attacked with their sticks.

YARGH!

CRACK!

CRUMP!

The dinosaur wobbled and toppled over. As it hit the floor, its head broke into pieces.

Darren stepped back. "I think we killed it!" he panted.

Bertie gasped. "It's not dead! It's a model – made of paper and stuff!"

They had really done it this time. Suddenly the door burst open.

"What do you think you're doing?" growled Mr Monk.

"Um ... we can explain," mumbled Bertie, backing away.

Mr Monk caught sight of the dinosaur. "My Tyrannosaurus!" he howled. He sunk to his knees with a moan. "It took me *weeks* to make this! It was going on display in Pudsley Museum!"

Bertie picked up a piece of green head. "Maybe you can glue it back together?" he said feebly.

Mr Monk glared. His face had gone purple, his moustache twitched. "YOU ... YOU VANDALS!" he snarled. "Wait till I get my hands on you!"

Bertie didn't wait. He fled down the stairs, with Darren and Eugene hot on his heels. Mr Monk chased them on to the street, where Angela was waiting.

"RUN!" yelled Bertie. "RUN!"

The three of them fled down the road, with Angela trying to catch up.

"Wait! WAIT FOR ME!" she wailed.

Eugene glanced over his shoulder. "He's still coming!" he gasped.

"Make for the park," panted Bertie. "We can hide in the trees!"

They dashed in through the gates and raced past the playground. Bertie plunged into the trees. He was running so fast, he forgot to look where he was going. Suddenly the ground gave way beneath him...

CRASH!

He landed in a hail of earth and branches. Seconds later Darren and Eugene fell on top of him.

"OWWW! OOOF!"

They sat up, struggling to untangle their arms and legs.

"What happened?" groaned Eugene.

"We've fallen in our trap!" cried Darren.

They looked up.

"I think we lost him," panted Eugene.

"Yes, but there's just one problem," said Bertie. "How are we going to get out?"

They looked at each other. The hole was deeper than Bertie remembered.

"ANG-ER-LA!" they yelled.

A head appeared, smiling down at them.

"Oh dear, are you stuck?" asked Angela.

"Of course we're stuck!" cried Bertie. "Help us out!"

Angela glanced back over her shoulder. Mr Monk was coming their way. "Sorry," she said. "I'm a bit busy right now..."

CHOCOLATE!

CHAPTER 1

Miss Boot stood in front of Class 3.

"As you know, our Spring Fair is this Saturday," she said. "Who's remembered to bring something for the stalls?"

Every hand went up – all except Bertie's because he was picking his nose. Miss Boot went round collecting toys, books, games, knitted booties and pots of jam. Know-All Nick handed her a box of white hankies.

"Thank you, Nicholas," said Miss Boot. "Bertie, what have you brought?"

"Uhh?" said Bertie.

He fished in his pocket and brought out a toothbrush.

"This is old," said Miss Boot. "It's been used."

"I know," said Bertie. "That's why I don't want it."

A voice sang out from the back of the class. "Miss Boot! You haven't asked me what *I've* brought!"

Everyone turned round. Bertie rolled his eyes. Trust Royston Rich to butt in. Royston was the world's biggest show-off. He'd probably brought in a signed photo of himself.

Royston placed a large box on his desk. Everyone gasped. It was the biggest Easter egg they'd ever seen.

Bertie stared at it, boggle-eyed. It was a whopper, bigger than a football … bigger even than Royston's big head.

"Splendid!" said Miss Boot, picking it up. "I think it's almost too good for the sweet stall."

"It ought to be a prize, Miss," said Donna.

"Ooh yes, we could have a competition!" cried Know-All Nick. "You have to guess the weight and whoever's closest wins the egg!"

Miss Boot nodded. "Do you know, Nicholas, I think that's a *brilliant* idea!"

Nick glowed with pride. Obviously it was a brilliant idea because he had thought of it. Better still, it meant he could get his hands on all that yummy chocolate. He was bound to win the competition because he always came first at everything.

At the back of the class, Bertie hadn't been able to take his eyes off the egg. *Imagine it*, he thought, *a chocolate egg so big you'd need a forklift truck to get it home*. Whatever it took, he had to win – and no one was going to stop him. Not even Know-All Nick.

By break time, word had spread round the whole school. Everyone was talking about the monster egg.

"I'd eat a little bit every day," said Eugene.

"It would last for months."

"It'd probably go mouldy," said Darren. "I'd eat it all in one day."

"I'd guzzle it in five minutes," said Bertie. "And then I'd be sick."

"What makes you think you'd get the chance?" sneered a voice.

Bertie swung round. It was that slimy sneak, Know-All Nick. He was always snooping on other people's conversations.

"Who asked you, big nose?" said Bertie.

Nick ignored him. "Face it," he said. "You're never going to win."

"Oh, yeah? Why not?" said Bertie.

"Because obviously *I'm* going to win," boasted Nick.

"Says who?"

"Says me!"

"We'll see about that," said Bertie. "I'm pretty good at guessing."

"Really?" said Nick. "But I won't need to guess because I'm a genius. I can work it out."

"How?" said Bertie.

Nick tapped his nose. "Ahh, wouldn't you like to know?" he smirked. "See you later, losers!"

Bertie watched him go. Right, he thought, *this means war. Only one of us can win that* egg. He couldn't wait to see the look on Nick's face when Miss Boot handed him the prize.

CHAPTER 2

All that morning Bertie couldn't stop thinking about the giant egg. Miss Boot had removed it from class because she was tired of people wanting to hold it. Everyone was desperate to guess how much it weighed.

Bertie sighed – he hadn't a clue. But what if Nick was telling the truth and you could work it out? Unfortunately, he was rubbish at maths. Subtraction was so tiring and fractions gave him a headache. No, if he was going to win he needed help. But who could he ask? Darren was no use. He got stuck on his three times table. And maths got Eugene muddled.

Hold on, thought Bertie, *if anyone knows the answer, it's Miss Boot*. She was a teacher after all! But how to trick her into giving him a clue? Bertie slipped out of his seat and made his way to the front.

"Miss," he said. "Can I ask a question?"

"No. Sit down," snapped Miss Boot. "Get on with your work."

"This is about work," said Bertie. "I was thinking about maths."

Miss Boot gawped. Was Bertie ill? Usually he avoided maths like the plague.

"Well, what is it?" she said.

"I was just wondering," said Bertie. "Are big things heavier than smaller things?"

Miss Boot sighed. "I've no idea what you're talking about."

"Well, like for instance, how much do *you* weigh?" asked Bertie.

"ME?" said Miss Boot.

"I don't mean exactly," said Bertie quickly. "I mean, roughly, do you weigh a ton or more?"

"A TON!" screeched Miss Boot, sounding as if she might explode. Bertie gulped. This wasn't going as well as he'd hoped.

"What about smaller things?" he babbled. "Like toffee or crisps or … chocolate eggs?"

Miss Boot's eyes narrowed. "Has this got something to do with a certain competition?"

"Erm, not really."

"Because let me warn you, Bertie, there will be *no cheating*," said Miss Boot. "If you think you can weigh that egg, forget it. It's somewhere you'll never find it. Now *sit down*."

Bertie trailed back to his seat. Some people were so suspicious. He hadn't got any information out of Miss Boot and now she suspected him of cheating.

He'd never even *thought* of weighing the egg. But actually that was a brilliant idea. If he could "borrow" it, he could find out the exact weight. There was just one problem. Where had Miss Boot hidden it? In her handbag? No, not big enough. The book cupboard? Too obvious.

A smile spread across Bertie's face. Of course! It was somewhere he'd never find it … somewhere children were not allowed… THE STAFFROOM!

CHAPTER 3

DRRRRINNG!

The bell rang for lunch break. Bertie shot out of class and flew down the corridor. He only had a minute to carry out his mission before the teachers arrived. He screeched to a halt at the staffroom and peeped round the door. No one was about.

Now ... where would Miss Boot hide a giant chocolate egg? He got down on all fours and looked under the coffee table. No luck. Nothing behind the curtains. His eye fell on the cupboard. He threw open the door. EUREKA! THERE IT WAS!

Bertie grabbed the monster egg. Now to weigh it... Argh! Bertie groaned. In his excitement he'd forgotten he'd need some scales.

Suddenly he heard voices in the corridor. Help! If Miss Boot caught him in the staffroom she'd go berserk.

Bertie looked around for somewhere to hide. But where? There was only the coffee table. It was a tight fit, but maybe he could squeeze underneath. He made it just as the door opened.

The room filled up with teachers. Bertie lay squashed under the table, not daring to breathe. This was like a horror film – trapped in a room with killer zombies! He could see Mr Weakly's shiny shoes and Miss Boot's baggy stockings only inches away.

"You know what Bertie asked me today?" Miss Boot was speaking.

"What?" asked Miss Darling.

"He asked me if I weighed a ton!"

Miss Darling giggled. "That boy! Tee hee!"

"He'll be the death of me," snorted Miss Boot. "Sometimes I think he lives on another planet."

"Sometimes I wish he did," said Mr Weakly.

Bertie almost banged his head. Was this what teachers talked about when they were alone? Him! Didn't they have homework to discuss?

MUNCH, MUNCH…

Bertie groaned. Now they were eating their sandwiches! He could smell cheese and pickle. This was torture. If only he'd brought something to eat!

Then he remembered – he had the chocolate egg. But there was no way he could touch that. It was a prize for the school fair. Miss Boot would blow a fuse. On the other hand, it was chocolate … and it was enormous… Who was going to miss a teeny-weeny piece?

Slowly, Bertie slid out the egg from its box. He peeled off the gold paper and broke off a piece. SNAP!

He held his breath. Luckily the teachers were too busy yakking to hear. Bertie crammed the chocolate into his mouth.

Mmm, mmm! It was the sweetest, smoothest chocolate he'd ever tasted. One more piece and then he'd put it away.

"Has anyone seen my glasses case?" It was Mr Weakly again.

Bertie looked about. By his feet was a blue glasses case.

"Maybe it's fallen on the floor?" suggested Miss Darling.

Bertie turned cold. If Mr Weakly bent down to look, he'd see him under the table. He had to do something and fast! He gave the glasses case a kick. It shot out from under the table. A moment later a hand reached down.

"It's all right. Found it!" cried Mr Weakly.

Bertie breathed out. That was close. He nibbled more chocolate to calm his nerves.

The lunch hour dragged on. Bertie's neck ached from lying squashed under the table. His hands were sweating. Only chocolate kept him going. At long last the bell rang.

Bertie waited until he was certain the last teacher had gone and crawled out.

There wasn't time to weigh the egg now. He had to put it back and return to class. He looked down and gasped.

YIKES! Who'd scoffed half the egg? He must have gobbled it without even knowing. What was he going to do?

Miss Boot would go bonkers if she found out. Bertie wrapped up the half-eaten egg and slid it back in the box. Wait a minute... Only the front half of the egg was showing, which still looked smooth and perfect. No one would guess! He was saved!

He stuffed the Easter egg back in the cupboard. Now to whizz back to class before Miss Boot missed him. He licked his lips. Hmm, first he'd better wipe the chocolate off his face.

CHAPTER 4

The day of the Spring Fair was bright and sunny. The school playground was crowded with people. Many of Bertie's class were in charge of stalls.

By far the most popular was the Giant Easter Egg competition run by Miss Boot. The egg stood proudly on the table in its gold box. People queued to pay fifty pence to guess the weight. Miss Boot's cash box was stuffed with coins and notes. In five minutes she had promised to announce the winner.

Bertie and his friends sucked lollipops as they watched.

"I never win anything," sighed Eugene.

"Someone has to win," said Darren.

Bertie shrugged. "It's only an Easter egg," he said.

"Are you kidding?" said Darren. "It's massive! It's the biggest chocolate egg in history!"

"Yes," said Eugene. "Imagine taking the first bite."

Well, maybe not the first, thought Bertie, *because I already scoffed half of it*. He hoped Miss Boot would hurry up. Maybe he'd be the winner? He'd made a guess like everyone else – there was no sense in not entering. Someone poked him in the back. Bertie turned round to see his enemy, Know-All Nick.

"I hope you're not going to cry, Bertie," he jeered.

"Cry?" said Bertie. "What for?"

"When I win the competition," said Nick.

"What makes you so sure?" asked Bertie.

"I told you," said Nick. "I'm a genius. I worked it out."

Miss Boot was heading to the microphone. Bertie joined the crowd to hear the result. Whoever won was in for a bit of a surprise. But he wasn't worried. No one could pin the blame on him.

"And now, the result of our Giant Easter Egg competition," said Miss Boot. "There were a huge number of entries but the winner is..." She looked up. "Nicholas!"

Bertie laughed. Who else? Know-All Nick wouldn't be smiling so much when he unwrapped his prize.

Nick made his way to the front as people clapped.

Miss Boot handed over the golden egg. "Well done, Nicholas," she said. "Your guess was exactly right."

"Huh, how amazing," said Bertie.

"Yeah," grumbled Darren. "I bet he cheated."

Nick made straight towards them, eager to enjoy his triumph. "I told you," he gloated. "I'm a genius!"

"You cheated," said Bertie.

"Not really," said Nick. "I used my brain. It turns out Spillers are selling this Easter egg in their shop. So I popped in and asked what it weighed."

"Like I said, you cheated," said Bertie.

Nick licked his lips. "Never mind, Bertie. As a special treat, you can watch me eat it."

"Now?" said Bertie.

"Why not?" said Nick. "I've got masses of chocolate, so I can eat it any time I like."

He slid the giant egg out of the box and greedily tore off the wrapper. His face turned a ghastly white.

"NOOOOOOOO!" he wailed. "SOMEONE'S EATEN IT!"

"No! Really?" said Bertie, trying not to smile.

Nick spun round to face him. Only one person could have done this. "YOU ATE IT!" he cried. "I'm telling!"

Bertie gave a shrug.

"But Nickerless, how could I?" he said. "Miss Boot had it locked away. No one could have touched that egg. Well, not unless they were a genius!"

PET SITTER!

CHAPTER 1

Bertie was in the kitchen doing his homework. He sighed loudly. How was he meant to concentrate when Mum and Mrs Nicely kept talking?

He hoped she hadn't come round to invite him to one of Angela's parties. Last time it had turned out to be just him and a dozen girls in fairy costumes.

"...So, we're going to my sister's for the weekend," Mrs Nicely was saying. "But I can't think what to do about Pusskins. Normally Mrs Crab feeds him, but she's in hospital."

"Oh dear," said Mum.

"Exactly," said Mrs Nicely. "I'm really in a fix. In fact, I was wondering if you might do it?"

"I'd be glad to," said Mum, "but I've got a lot on this weekend. What about Bertie?"

"ME?" Bertie looked up from doodling a picture of Miss Boot.

Mrs Nicely frowned. She was hoping to find someone sensible. Bertie was about as sensible as a jelly sandwich.

"Well, I don't know," she said doubtfully. "Are you good with cats?"

"Not especially," said Bertie. "I'm good with dogs."

Bertie didn't mind cats, but he didn't really see the point of them. All they did was sleep, laze around and eat. You couldn't take a cat for a walk or throw a ball for it to fetch. Pusskins was too fat and idle to fetch anything. Anyway, he didn't see why he had to feed him.

Mrs Nicely sighed. "Well, it would be doing me a great favour. And, of course, I'd pay you."

"PAY ME?" cried Bertie. "How much?"

"BERTIE!" groaned Mum.

"It's all right," said Mrs Nicely. "Let's see, what about five pounds?"

FIVE POUNDS? Bertie almost fell off his chair. That was more than double his pocket money! And all for feeding a fat moggy. Yippee! He was going to be rich!

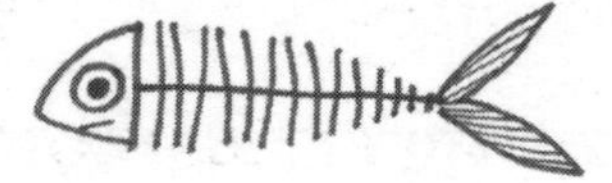

Bertie followed Mrs Nicely next door so she could explain what he had to do. Angela was in the kitchen practising her ballet. She ran upstairs and came back with Pusskins, who lolled in her arms like a furry pudding.

"Here he is!" she trilled. "This is Bertie. Say hello, Pusskins."

Bertie reached out a hand.

"Grrrrr!" snarled the cat, arching his back.

"He likes having his tummy tickled," said Angela. "You have to feed him twice a day and he only likes Kitty Krunch."

Fusspot, thought Bertie. Whiffer would eat anything – even the pizza off your plate.

"When does he go out?" he asked.

"After tea and only in the back garden," said Angela. "Mostly he sleeps on my bed, don't you, Pussypops?"

Mrs Nicely showed Bertie the cat food and gave him a front door key.

"One more thing," she said. "Don't forget to turn off the burglar alarm."

"Burglar alarm?" said Bertie. No one had mentioned this before! Mrs Nicely showed him a panel by the door with rows of buttons.

"It's quite simple," she said. "You just punch in the code to turn it on or off – four-two-seven. Can you remember that?"

Bertie nodded.

"Repeat it to me."

"Four … seven … umm…"

Mrs Nicely rolled her eyes. "I'll write it down for you," she said. "And lock the door when you leave. Have you got all that?"

"Yes," said Bertie. "Do the alarm, feed the cat and lock the door."

"Don't forget," warned Mrs Nicely. "The alarm's linked to the police station so it must be turned off immediately."

She watched Bertie stuff the key in his pocket. Possibly she was out of her mind – this was, after all, the boy who'd arrived at Angela's party dressed as a worm. But it was too late to find someone else. All he had to do was feed a cat – surely even Bertie could manage that?

CHAPTER 2

BEEP! BEEP! BEEP!

It was Saturday morning. Bertie had let himself in to the Nicelys' house and the burglar alarm was going mad. *ARGH! Quick! Where's that piece of paper?* He found it in his pocket and hurriedly punched in the code.

BEEP! BEEP! BE— The alarm stopped.

Bertie let out a sigh of relief. Why did the Nicelys need a burglar alarm anyway? Why didn't they just get a guard dog?

He went into the kitchen and filled the cat bowl with Kitty Krunch.

"PUSSKINS!" he called. "Look what I've got!"

The fat grey cat appeared in the doorway and plodded into the kitchen. It glared at Bertie then sniffed the food as if it might be rat poison. Bertie glanced around the kitchen – suddenly it dawned on him that he had the Nicelys' house all to himself. He could do whatever he liked! He could watch TV with his feet up or help himself to biscuits. He could bounce on all the beds. Come to think of it, he'd never seen Angela's bedroom. Maybe he'd have a quick nose around.

Bertie crept upstairs. Angela's bedroom had pink walls with pink curtains and a pink duvet covered in hearts.

YUCK! thought Bertie. He flopped on to the bed. Wouldn't Angela be furious if she could see him now? It would serve her right for telling everyone he was her boyfriend. He looked at Angela's books. They had titles like *My Cuddly Kitten Gets Lost and Girls 4 Ever!* He took down a sparkly exercise book. On the cover were the words: MY STORIES by Angela Nicely – Strickly Private.

Ah ha! thought Bertie. What was so private that Angela didn't want anyone reading it? He opened the book at the first story.

Once upon a time there was a beautiful princess called Princess Angela. She lived in a big palace with loads of servants to make her bed and turn on the TV and stuff.

One sunny day Princess Angela was playing in her garden when a prince came by. His name was Prince Bertie and secretly he had falled in love with Princess Angela…

WHAT?! Bertie threw the book down in disgust. He wanted to be sick. How dare Angela put him in her soppy fairy tale? How dare she make him a drippy prince who went round falling in love and living happily ever after?

What if any of his friends saw the story? Bertie felt ill. What if Angela ever read it out in class? The news would be all round school in no time. People would start calling him Prince Bertie! YUCK!

No, he had to make sure that didn't happen. But how? He could throw the book in the dustbin. But wait, he had a better idea. Why not simply change the story? He could cross out his own name and replace it with someone else – Prince Nickerless for example.

Bertie smiled to himself. Wouldn't Angela be mad when she saw it? He glanced at the clock. Mum would be wondering where he was. Never mind, he'd carry out his brilliant plan later when he gave Pusskins his tea.

CHAPTER 3

BEEP! BEEP! BEEP!

The burglar alarm rang out. It was six o'clock and Bertie was back. As he hurried inside, something shot through his legs like a furry rocket. ARGH! Pusskins had got out! Bertie was just in time to see him vanish over the wall. This was terrible!

Pusskins wasn't meant to go out the front. What if he went missing – or got run over? Mrs Nicely would blame him. Angela would burst into tears, and he could forget about his five pounds.

BEEP! BEEP! The alarm could wait – he had to find that pesky cat. He looked over next-door's wall. "Pusskins! Puss puss!"

No sign of him. Bertie searched up and down the road.

"Pusskins!"

Nothing. He dashed back to the house.

Pusskins was sitting on the doormat, yawning.

Bertie gave him a look.

BEEP! BEEP!

What was that noise? It sounded like … HELP! – THE BURGLAR ALARM! What was the number? *Two … four … umm…?* Bertie fumbled in his pocket for the piece of paper and punched in the code. The alarm stopped.

He stood panting for breath. It was a close thing but everything seemed okay. Pusskins slunk past him into the kitchen.

Bertie poured out the Kitty Krunch, then hurried upstairs. Angela's storybook was still on the bed. Now to make a few small changes…

Once upon a time there was a SMELLY ~~beautiful~~ princess called Princess POOPALOT ~~Angela~~. She lived in a big DUSTBIN ~~palace~~ with loads of RATS AND MAGGOTS ~~servants~~ to make her bed and turn on the TV and stuff.

One sunny day Princess POOPALOT ~~Angela~~ was playing in her garden when a prince came by. His name was Prince NICKERLESS THE UGLY ~~Bertie~~ and secretly he had falled in A COWPAT ~~love with Princess Angela~~…

Bertie broke off. What was that noise? It sounded like it came from downstairs. It was probably only Pusskins. He went back to his story.

SLAM!

Bertie froze. Not even Pusskins could slam a door. Help! There was someone in the house. Bertie gulped. What was the use of a burglar alarm if a burglar could just walk in?

CHAPTER 4

Bertie looked around in panic. If he tried to sneak downstairs the burglar might hear him. If only he had his trusty pirate cutlass. But all Angela had in her room was teddies and cuddly rabbits. He grabbed *The Bedtime Book of Fairy Tales*, which was the biggest book on the shelf. Voices were coming from downstairs.

"Find anything?"

"No, nothing."

Bertie broke into a cold sweat. There wasn't one burglar, but two! Maybe if he kept very quiet the crooks wouldn't come upstairs.

CLUMP, CLUMP, CLUMP...

Uh oh. Bertie looked round for somewhere to hide. He slipped behind Angela's bedroom door and held his breath. Footsteps came along the landing.

"You take that one, I'll check in here."

CREAK!

The bedroom door swung back, squashing him against the wall. A big man came into the room. Bertie crept out and raised the book above his head...

THWACK!

"OWW!"

The man fell flat on his face. Bertie stared at his uniform.

"You're the police!" he gasped.

"Of course I'm the police," said the constable. "Oww! That really hurt!"

A sergeant came rushing in.

"He hit me!" grumbled the constable.

"Don't be so soft," said the sergeant. He gripped Bertie's arm. "Right, young man, you'd better come along with us," he said sternly.

"What for?" said Bertie.

"For breaking into this house."

"But I didn't!"

"You set off the burglar alarm. Didn't you hear it?" asked the sergeant.

Bertie stared. Mrs Nicely's words came back to him: the burglar alarm was linked to the police station. He should have turned it off straight away. Now the police thought he was a burglar!

"But I only came to feed the cat!" he protested.

The sergeant laughed. "That's a good one. So why were you hiding?"

"Because I thought *you* were burglars!" wailed Bertie.

"Very funny," said the sergeant. "We'll talk about this at the station."

At the station! *This is a nightmare*,

thought Bertie. *I'll be sent to prison! I'll never see Whiffer again!*

The policemen took him downstairs and outside to the police car.

"That's my house, next door!" cried Bertie.

"Of course it is!" laughed the sergeant, shaking his head.

"No, really, it is!" yelled Bertie. "You can ask my mum!"

The policemen looked at each other. The boy did seem a bit young for a burglar. Maybe it was best to be on the safe side. They rang the doorbell.

Mum came to the door. Her eyes almost popped out of her head when she saw Bertie with two policemen.

"Sorry to bother you, madam. Do you know this boy?" asked the sergeant.

"I should do," said Mum. "He's my son. What's he done now?"

Bertie threw back his head. "NOTHING!" he howled. "THAT'S WHAT I KEEP TELLING THEM!"

It took about half an hour and two cups of tea to explain the whole story. Luckily, the sergeant saw the funny side. He said that in future Bertie should be kept away from burglar alarms. And he better not make a habit of belting policemen over the head.

When they'd gone, Mum rounded on him. "I thought you knew how to work the alarm!" she fumed.

"I did!" said Bertie. "It was Pusskins's fault. He ran off!"

Mum folded her arms. "Well, I don't know what Mrs Nicely will say," she said.

"She doesn't have to know, does she?" said Bertie.

"No," said Mum grimly. "Maybe we'll keep it that way."

On Sunday the Nicelys returned. Mrs Nicely came round with Angela.

"Thank you so much for feeding Pusskins," she said. "I hope everything was all right?"

"Um, yes, fine," mumbled Bertie.

"Good. And no problems with the burglar alarm?"

Bertie looked at Mum.

"No, no problems at all," she said.

"Marvellous!" said Mrs Nicely. "Well, thank you, Bertie, you've been a great help."

She stuffed something into his hand and went on chatting. Bertie looked. A five-pound note! He could buy hundreds of—

EH? The money was grabbed from his hand.

"I'll take that, thank you," said Angela.

"W-what?" said Bertie. "But it's mine!"

Angela shook her head. "I need a new storybook," she said. "Someone scribbled in mine."

"Oh, did they?" said Bertie.

Angela narrowed her eyes. "Don't be stupid. I know it was you."

Bertie sighed. He should have seen this coming. "Okay, I'll make a deal," he said. "Half each."

Angela shook her head. "No thanks! I'll keep it all. Unless you want me to tell my mum."

Bertie's shoulders drooped. He knew when he was beaten. In future he was having nothing to do with cats.

"Oh, by the way," said Angela, on her way out. "I'm starting on a new story. It's called Bertie Ballerina!"

Out now: